RAISE UP, HEART

by
Leta Blake

An Original Publication from Leta Blake Books

Raise Up, Heart

Written by Leta Blake
Cover by Cate Ashwood Designs
Formatted by BB eBooks

First Print Edition, 2020
ISBN: 979-8-88841-067-7

Hearts don't lie.

Two years ago, grief took Cole's heart when he lost Damon, the love of his life in an accident. He's felt empty ever since. But his lover's heart survives, placed inside his cousin, Alex.

As time passes, it becomes clear: Damon's heart is too devoted to Cole. It's strong, and lovelorn, and terrifyingly true blue. The fight for Alex's body is brutal. But, to win, Damon's heart only has to beat.

Ba-boom. Ba-boom.

Even faced with the horror of his lover's eerie return, Cole's heart leaps at the chance to finally have the man he's yearned for. What will he sacrifice to be with Damon? And who will pay the ultimate price?

Raise Up, Heart, is a stand-alone, second chance gay romance, inspired by the famous gothic, short stories of yore. With head nods to Edgar Allen Poe and Mary Shelley's *Frankenstein, Raise Up, Heart*, is dark, epic, consuming, and dreamlike. Released just in time for Halloween, the story includes angst, steam, and a happy ending. This novella displays Leta Blake's writing style at its most beautiful and challenging.

For the Poe fan in me and
the gothic heart in you

PROLOGUE

POE CAN SPEAK to you of hearts: the ticking of them, the secrets within; he knows their ferocious strength. Poe understands. Hearts can't be tucked beneath the floorboard of a house. They will not rest there, complicit and quiet. He knows they are stronger than that, louder, greedier—vengeful. He knows that a heart can come back for you, take you over, take you apart. It only has to beat. Ba-boom. Ba-boom. And within that sound there is infinity, and within infinity there resides the untold and unspeakable. These stories of Poe's, you'll never believe them, though they may chill you through. Yet they are true all the same.

True like a darling heart is true blue.

IT BEGINS WITH a sandwich. The bread is spongy beneath your fingers, the meat slippery and cold from the refrigerator, and the squirt of the mustard satisfyingly perverse. So you add a slap of mayo to lighten the mood and you take a bite, closing your eyes, chewing slowly, savoring the taste that you've almost forgotten how to enjoy.

It progresses when your girlfriend Emily lets loose a soft sound, and you open your eyes to look at her, all vanilla, warm, haloed in the light from the kitchen. "Are you okay?"

"Are you?" she asks, bright eyes glancing between your sandwich and your mustard-smeared mouth. Her frown stirs a restlessness in you.

"Of course." You sense it down deep, how very okay you are now that you can breathe again. Your cousin Damon Black's heart is in your chest, pumping your blood, and stirring the life inside you. Yes, relentless grief aside, you're feeling physically better than you have since the accident. "Why?"

"The sandwich," Emily says. "Damon…he… When we were in high school together, he ate his sandwiches just like that. Mustard, mayo, stacked with sandwich meat. You used to joke that it'd give him a coronary, remember?"

The words are in the air between you, the tension horrible, and you let them hang.

And you feel guilty. Of course you do. You've felt guilty every day since you discovered the source of the new heart beating in your chest. It never stops. You think you should throw the sandwich away, toss it into the trash, and make Emily forget you're holding so much sadness. But she loves you. You see it in her eyes, the way she looks at you like you're too good to be true, and you feel it in the way she takes you in her arms at night, tremulous and tender.

"Go on, eat it," Emily whispers. "I think you should. Damon would want you to."

So you do. You take bites of the sandwich and truly taste each flavor. It's true you've put on more mustard than usual. True you've never been a fan of ham. But here, right now, in your kitchen, enveloped in the fuzz of relief and a second chance at life, you know you owe Damon more than you could ever hope to pay.

And you'd give anything for a chance pay him back. So you eat the sandwich.

For Damon.

IT NEXT SHOWS itself when you're walking through town. You see three old men huddled around a table playing chess. Though you never liked the game, preferring to run a football in the backyard with your friends any day of the week, you find yourself attracted to the glint of the shiny white and black pieces in the mid-autumn sun. You wander over, because after such a close brush with death, you will never deny yourself simple pleasures again.

You watch one of the men touch a pawn, and you can't say how you know that he's making a mistake, but you tell him, "You don't want to do that."

He removes his finger and says, "You're right, son. Good eye you have there." He points at another piece, more decorated and slimmer. "That would leave my queen in jeopardy."

You nod and feel a sense of *rightness* settle over you as the man goes back to contemplating the checkered board. There's a flash of light out of the corner of your eye. The sun has fallen on the glass windows of the stores across the street, and you see a scarf that makes you think of Emily, so you leave the men and head inside the store.

"Alex," the shop keep greets you.

You're certain that you know her name, but it isn't coming to you, so you incline your head and smile boyishly, hoping that it gets you by. They've told you, and well you know, there may be some lapses in memory due to the trauma to your body and brain sustained after the accident.

The scarf is soft, silken, and it runs through your fingers like Emily's hair. You know that she'll like it, and you skim it through your hand again.

Soft, short, fistful.

You shake your head, confused, and rub at your eyes. The scarf flutters to the floor, and you bend to pick it up, placing it back on the table, leaving without purchasing it.

You go home and sit on the sofa, clutching a pillow

to your chest. You think about the chess game, the scarf, the shock of some odd memory that you can feel still against your palm but can't recall from any part of your life. You sit so still and so quiet that you count the thud of your pulse in your neck and notice the gentle shaking of your torso as Damon's heart beats in your chest.

Emily comes home, all smiles and open arms. You steal a kiss from her lovely lips and whisper to her, "I'm so grateful to be here with you."

It's a beautiful world, despite the pain. You know how precious each moment is now that you've been given this second chance at life.

So, at night, before bed, you take the time to smell Emily's perfume when the bottle catches your eye on the bathroom counter. Then you carefully fold the toothpaste tube from the bottom, though you never have before, because it feels right. And as the moon rises outside the window, you climb into bed with the woman of your dreams.

EMILY IS RIDING you, heaving up and down while you're lost in her wet goodness. Her breasts are sweet, supple globes in your hands, and you lean up to kiss her neck.

Stubble, sharp, scratchy, hot on your lips.

You jerk back, and blink at Emily, taking in her face twisted in a moment of bliss. Your stomach goes into knots.

Emily doesn't notice, and you close your eyes, because this is always so sweet now, such a joy to let your body feel this beautiful bliss—

Tight, hot, gripping, and a guttural male groan.

—"Oh, God," you cry, covering your face with your hands, trying to block whatever memory has ripped into your mind.

"Oh, God, Alex!" Emily echoes, speeding up her movements. "Oh, it's so good, baby. So good," she croons, and you have to fight to keep from shoving her off and away.

You focus on your cock sliding wetly in and out and send a desperate prayer up to the heavens because you are suddenly terrified that you simply won't be able to pull this off.

That she'll sense…that she'll know….

Her body clenches at you and you jerk under her, hoping that she doesn't notice that the condom is empty, hoping that when she pulls off, she thinks you've come, too.

You slide away fast, kissing her mouth, kissing her hair, saying, "I need to clean up. I'm tired." Then you want to bite your own tongue because now she's going to worry that you've strained Damon's heart. "It's okay. I just…I need to get some rest. It was good, Emily," you say. "You're so good, so beautiful in every way."

You throw the condom away, and your cock wilts in

your hand. You run the water. Splash it on your face, and stare at yourself in the mirror. The red scar down the center of your chest is violent and still new. You run your finger over the seam, thinking of being cracked open, the bloody, red and white mess of it all. You shudder when you think of them ripping open Damon's body to harvest his heart for you.

"Alex?" Emily asks from the doorway. Her night-gown is white and sheer, her gentle outline visible beneath it, and you want to go to her, to wrap your arms around her. You want to tell her all the odd things you've felt lately, all the memories you can't explain. But you don't. Because her grief for her friend—your cousin—and her fear for you is still too fresh. And this is all too confusing.

And, perhaps, if you're lucky, it will simply go away.

If you're lucky.

IT ESCALATES WHEN you see Cole Hart at the hospital. You're there for a check-up. You're still on leave until you're more fully healed, and though you've felt up to returning to your job as a nurse practitioner in a family practice for a week or more now, Emily won't hear of it.

Cole is there for some sort of business, he's dressed in nice clothes and he has a bundle of files in his hands, paperwork of some kind, and he looks lost. You watch as he stops in the middle of the hallway, his eyes going distant and strange.

You know, you understand, and you've felt it too—Dr. Damon Black should be here, and you want him to be. You expect that at any point, around any corner, the nurses will be scurrying away from his commanding voice. Damon had been the kind of doctor who came at his job with all the sheer force of his will.

You are just about to call out to Cole, to greet him, when his lips twist with grief, and he brings the back of his hand to his mouth, holding back tears. It isn't fair that he lost Damon. They didn't have enough time together. It isn't fair that you're alive when Damon is gone. Cole sobs softly and you freeze.

Pain, breathless violent, soul-rending pain.

The world goes black around you, and you taste blood in your mouth.

"Oh, God, Alex! Are you—? Someone! We need help!"

It's Cole. His hands are on you, and you grab hold of them, holding them to your chest, as you stare up at him, feeling as wild-eyed as he looks. He's in a panic now, his tears are still wet on his face and his breathing comes unnaturally fast.

His lips are red and open, and he's saying something to you, and you want him to keep talking.

"Alex, what's wrong? Is it his heart?"

The clatter of feet on the hospital floor, and the soft

thud of knees and legs hit the ground beside you, as Cole is pulled back, *away*. And you're stuck being checked by a man who introduces himself as Dr. Jones and three nurses, all of them touching you at once. Cole stands to the side of the hospital bed you've somehow landed in, his arms crossed over his chest, with his eyes wrecked and vulnerable.

"How's my heart?" you whisper, as the monitors beep away.

Across the room, Cole flinches.

Your heart? Or is it Damon's heart?

Honestly, you no longer know.

EMILY HOLDS AN ice pack to your lip and runs her fingers through your hair soothingly. The hospital has summoned her despite your assurances that it's unnecessary, that you're fine, and it was just a strange, sudden blackout.

Even as you say the words, you know that they aren't convincing: a recent heart transplant patient falling on his face, busting his lip, with only a report of a strange, intense pain to explain it, is not apt to be sent along home without a battery of tests being run. You know that, and you accept it. Any resistance has left you for good, drummed out of you by Damon's heart and replaced with a deep, painful shame.

You also know that it's more than that. You sit in the hospital gown, your hands crossed in your lap, and Emily hovers by your side. You try not to think of how Cole had stood beside your bed ten minutes ago, messy blond hair aglow and eyes red with tears. You try not to remember how he *commanded* you to get well, saying, "It's his heart. It's all that's left of him. Do this for me. Please."

Emily says, "Are you feeling better? You're so quiet."

You sigh and shrug. "I'm okay." You try to sound jovial. "Just a little wounded pride is all."

Emily is unconvinced, and her fingers twine into your hair, taking the short strands into her fist.

Fistful, short, and soft. Cole's soft sigh as you command him.

You shiver hard.

Emily puts the ice pack down and turns fully to you, carding both her hands through your hair, messing it.

"So strange," she says softly.

"What?" you ask. Have you said it aloud? The memories that assault you as sensation—have they translated into words?

"Your hair," she murmurs. "It's…different."

You attempt a chuckle, a shock of panic jolting you. "Different? I need a cut, if that's what you mean."

"No… it's…" Emily shakes her head. "Never mind. It's silly. It's nothing. More than that," she says cheerily. "It's impossible."

Your false smile fades even more. "Just tell me," you

say.

She shrugs, shakes her head a little, and scrunches up her face in an endearing way, and messes with your hair again. "It's just coming in wavy is all, and kind of strawberry-gold? It sort of... looks like Damon's."

You swallow and nod. Somehow, this is what you are expecting.

YOU FEEL CLAUSTROPHOBIC in your own skin, like it doesn't belong to you. You fight the urge to claw at yourself, wanting to find a way out. You've never been so uncomfortable in your life, not even after the accident, not even when you thought you were dying and you couldn't get a good breath. No, this is so much more intense than that, a wrongness that feels soul deep, and you have to escape this cage you're trapped in, or...

Or you'll die in it.

On other days, it's quite the opposite. You feel like you *are* the cage, and there's a vicious animal trying to rip its way out. It starts as a pain in your chest. The doctors confirm, though, that your—no, *Damon's*—heart is fine. There's no sign of rejection, or inflammation, or fluid. There's nothing to explain the pain you're feeling. You see it in their eyes. It's all in your head.

The pain consumes you. It moves to your stomach and radiates through to your back. It's suffocating, like nothing you've ever felt before. Painkillers don't even make a dent, though you pop them to deal with the emotions that you can't handle. This is supposed to be your new life. You and Emily moving into a future so bright that it makes you squint.

But no—instead, you're steadily losing it all.

There are days when time seems to expand and contract, and sometimes you find yourself missing hours. The men who play chess in the park know you now, and they call you "Sir Chess Master" as you pass by, but you can't remember ever playing a single game with them. Hell, you barely even remember the rules.

The most terrifying moments are when you see Cole. You've started to hide in the bedroom when he comes to visit Emily at the house. They've become such good friends now, almost as close as she and Damon had been, and you can't deny him the comfort he needs from her. But even his voice causes you so much pain that you sweat at the sound of it. The monster inside you becomes all claws and teeth, and if Cole cries—if they talk about Damon and you hear his voice break—then you have to tear into the pillow with your teeth to hold back the screams.

Emily is hurt. You see how she fights to be close to you, but you can't bear to have her in the same room when you're suffering. She can't see this. She can't know how you're losing this battle, how you don't even know how to begin to fight. Unless you plunge your hand inside and rip the heart from your chest, you know the monster will win.

It's not like you haven't considered doing just that.

Over time, the walls close in on you. You can't escape what's inside. You can't get rid of the thing that's killing you. Your hair changes color entirely. You find half-eaten sandwiches that you don't remember making. Your feet shrink and flop around inside your shoes. You lose so much weight that you have to buy new clothes. You stop looking like you. Your jawline narrows. Your skin is changing hue.

There comes a day when you wake up and Damon's eyes are peering back at you.

That is when you are no longer you, and you know that you can't stop what's happening. So you run, trying to go faster than wind, trying to outrun the heart enveloped in your skin.

CHAPTER 1

Raise Up, Heart

HEARTS ARE MESSY things. Gory, even, Cole would say. They beat and they break and they get carved out of chests and handed over to other people—who take off with that precious gift and leave only a note. A crazy, wild note that makes everyone doubt not only their heart but their sanity.

Yes, Cole knows hearts. And for the most part, he doesn't want anything to do with anyone's but his own. He doesn't like to think of himself as bitter, though. Mainly because he suspects that Damon would disapprove, and for some reason Cole still wants Damon's approval. Not that Damon disapproved of *bitterness*, per se; he seemed to embrace that well enough himself. But rather Cole knew deep down that Damon had loved him, at least in part, because he was not bitter, and Cole was loath to make himself unlovable to Damon even in his own memory.

Still, it had been two years since Alex had disappeared, leaving Emily wounded to the core, and leaving

Cole angry and helpless, grieving again as though Damon had just died.

Even before he left, Cole sometimes raged to himself about Alex, cursing that he'd been the one to survive the car accident, despite having been the one behind the wheel. He'd let himself think in uncharitable, if truthful, moments that if Alex had done *anything* differently that night, then Damon would still be here. He'd still be stalking around Maryville proclaiming it po'dunk, still looking at Cole like he wanted to eat him alive, like he could taste him just by breathing the air. Even so, despite being angry, Cole had also taken comfort in Alex's life and the knowledge that Damon's heart still beat inside of him, the living tissue of the man Cole loved with a strength undampened by death and time.

But two years ago, just a few months after the accident, Alex began to show signs of slipping, and they all noticed it. He changed. It started slowly. Whatever it was had twisted him up into knots, making him lose weight in a way that was wrong, like an elephant shedding fat to reveal a giraffe. And he grew strange, distant. Avoiding people whenever he could. Survivor's guilt, the doctor had told Emily. Survivor's guilt, Emily had echoed to Cole.

Patience didn't change anything, kindness just seemed to agitate the symptoms, and, after a while, Alex became entirely reclusive, closing himself up in the home he shared with Emily, acting paranoid and odd. He'd been scheduled to have a psych eval—Emily had insisted on it—just days before he fled. But he'd skipped it and then town, leaving a note that wildly stated, "It's making me go. I can't stop it. I'm so sorry. Goodbye."

Six months of investigations and searches, traces on all sales of anti-rejection drugs in the area, and endless prayers were fruitless. Nothing led to Alex. Not a word. Not a letter. And Emily had torn her heart out with grief while Cole held her, sobbing himself, broken to lose the last piece of Damon that he could track.

That was two years ago, and now Emily sits across from him in Southern Grace Coffee with fragile smile and a question: "Do I hope? Do I dare?"

Hearts are messy things. They run rampant and wild. Cole has seen this his whole life, the way his father's heart strayed, running all over town, and his family's hearts were broken by divorce. He wants to tell Emily to be careful, to keep her heart safe, but she's not him, and she never will be—and maybe he shouldn't keep his heart safe, either. How many times have they had *that* discussion? Emily saying, "Damon would want this. He'd want you to be happy."

But happy and hearts are, for Cole, not words that go together. Not now, anyway. It seems he's become even more difficult to please, finding practically everyone too *something* to invest in—too young, too innocent, too hopeful. Too much like someone who's never watched the man they love die from injuries from a senseless, violent car accident, and then signed the papers to have his heart ripped from his chest and put into the man who was driving the car. A man who then took it away from Cole forever and might be dead himself at this point.

Oh, no, these young men who ask Cole on dates, and even some of the older ones, are in no way prepared to deal with him. Cole isn't even prepared to deal with himself.

"Of course, Emily," Cole says. "Alex has been gone a long time. You deserve this. You should be happy."

"It just feels scary, you know?" Emily gazes at him, grips his hand tightly. "How do I know I can trust him? Do I even trust myself? Can I?"

"You can," Cole says, nodding, and smiling with as much love and encouragement as he can muster. "You're strong and amazing, and I have no doubt at all that Michael loves you. Have you seen the way he looks at you? He practically floats away."

Emily presses her lips together, trying to squash her smile, but her eyes are alight. "He does, doesn't he?"

"He does," Cole agrees, smiling with the joy that Emily won't allow herself. "And what's more, he's a *good* man, Emily."

Cole should know. He's hired Michael Saint John be the director of Appalachian Rainbows, one of the charities Cole set up with Damon's insurance money. It specializes in helping LGBT kids have safer school experiences. That leaves more time for Cole to work with Hardiest Hearts, a group focused on helping kids who are waiting for organ donors. In Cole's darkest hours, of which there are still too many, the kids keep him going; thinking of their fierce determination in the face of so much difficulty and tragedy allows Cole to find a similar determination in himself.

Michael and Cole have worked closely together for the last year. He's kind, generous, and incredibly good at his job. Not to mention, hiring Michael Saint John, getting to know and trust him, has allowed Cole to begin to truly dedicate himself to figuring out what to do with the family business he's been gifted from his grandfather: Hart Trucking.

As his mother keeps reminding him during her transcontinental phone calls, it's time to do one's business or get off the pot as far as that company goes, and Cole knows it. He can either grow Hart Trucking back up to the status it held before his grandfather's scandal, or he can chop it up and sell it. It's time to make a choice and not just let his grandfather's hand-picked men run the place with a little oversight from Cole to make sure they keep it all kosher.

Emily takes a deep breath and says, "Okay. I'll do it. I'll tell Michael yes."

"Wait," Cole says. "Yes, what?"

"I'll tell him that I'm ready to give it a try."

Cole says, "You'll...sleep with him?"

Emily gives him a silly, naughty look. "Why, Cole

Hart, I never thought you'd be nosey about the goings on in my bedroom."

"I just…recommend that you, I mean," Cole says, stumbling over what is still so hard to say. "I mean, I guess I'm saying don't make him wait."

Emily's eyes soften and she says, "Damon didn't mind waiting for you."

Cole rolls his eyes. "He minded. Believe me, he minded. Hell, *I* minded, but I was stupid and scared. I wish every day I'd had sex with him before he died."

Cole knows the stereotype of gay men: randy and promiscuous, easy and indiscriminate. But he's never been that way. He's still a virgin and he's only ever wanted to venture into the that kind of intimacy with someone he's willing to be entirely vulnerable with. After the way his grandfather used him when he was small, he's always been unwilling to expose himself fully even to Damon. They'd only been together for a year, and while their love had grown out of control like wildfire, Cole had wanted to make their first time perfect. He'd wanted to be sure physical intimacy with Damon could be managed without any bad memories coming up for him in the middle of it. No matter how gentle Cole had known Damon would be—despite his acerbic personality outside of the bedroom—he'd still wanted to be fully recovered emotionally before opening himself up to Damon like that. And he'd wanted his body to be perfect, too—twenty pounds lighter and more ripped.

So, he'd put sex on hold, never going beyond kisses and groping, never letting Damon touch him below the waist.

He's way more than twenty pounds lighter now. Grief and regret make for a killer diet. And now his fears of opening up before he's ready have been superseded by something worse: complete utter loss. He'd do anything to go back in time and do it all again.

Cole swallows hard and goes on. "If you're sure you want to make a go of it with Michael, then don't be shy, okay. Just show him how you feel. All the way."

Emily kisses his hand then and pats it ferociously. "You *will* love again, Cole," she says, like it's an order.

Cole just smiles, and he doesn't believe it.

On most days, Cole is fine. He smiles and laughs at jokes, and he works hard. He goes to weddings, and birthday parties, and he's certain not to be the grieving elephant in the room. On most days, sure, he thinks about Damon, but it only hurts like he guesses it should—it doesn't take his breath away and make him want to curl up and die. That's on most days.

Then there are other days, and those days hit hard.

The anniversary of Damon's death isn't too bad. Both years he's gone to visit his brother Gibson and his wife Jo and their new little scamp, his nephew, Max, a few days beforehand. That way he avoids the weird sinking sensation he sometimes gets, the one that says it hasn't happened yet, and it's about to happen now. That says he can still stop it.

It usually happens when the light is just right, and he steps out of his rented house in Maryville and walks toward his car. The light hits the trees at an exact angle, and he feels his heart stop and then throb. The world around him screams, the sky is caves in, and he can taste the clouds of it in his mouth, because it hasn't happened yet, and it's going to happen again. He has to grab hold of something just to keep from falling down with the weight of his panic, fear, and grief. And then it passes, and he stands up, and, if he *has* fallen, he brushes himself off.

Sometimes, on those days, he doesn't go anywhere. He just goes back inside after about fifteen minutes and stares at the bottles of liquor in his cabinet, and he stares at them some more. Then he curses the promises he's made, because it can be easy enough to drink until he hits the ground. Hits the ground, and tastes dirt, and chokes to death on his grief.

But then he remembers how Damon loved him, and he doesn't want to be a man that Damon wouldn't love. So he steps away from the bottles, and curls up on his sofa, and screams. Sometimes it's the only thing that will make the terrible longing go away.

But that isn't every day. Not even most days. Thank goodness. Because if that insanity comes over him too often, Cole isn't sure he won't go mad entirely. And he's already come back from that brink once. He doesn't think he can do it again.

Yes, on most days he simply goes to work with Hardier Hearts, and he keeps Hart Trucking running, and he talks with Michael more and more about what they want to do with Appalachian Rainbows. Sometimes, he heads over to Maryville Billiards to shoot a game of pool. And there have been nights when he sees someone, who, from a distance, looks like Damon, and his heart thump-thumps, and he has a moment of thinking maybe, just maybe…

Until he approaches and he's close enough to see that, no, the guy really isn't anything like Damon at all.

And then Cole leaves, goes home, and waits for the next day to happen, because it will. Time doesn't seem to ever stop.

"Thanks, Cole," Emily says. "You've been a real help. A true friend."

Cole waves at Emily as she leaves Southern Grace en route to what, Cole hopes, will be her happy ending. Emily deserves one, he thinks. Everyone does.

As he stands up, he throws a few bills on the table to tip the barista and then winds his scarf around his neck carefully. It's cold out, and he intends to walk back to his rented house on Indiana Avenue. It's almost Halloween, and the sun has been down for hours. Not a cloud and not a star in the sky, just seamless black that stretches above him as he walks. It's a pretty good distance from Southern Grace Coffee's to his house, full of busy roads. But sometimes walking clears his mind.

He pulls one glove off and stuffs his hand into his coat pocket, feeling the smooth, heart-shaped stone he carries there. It is almost two inches long and an inch and a half wide. He's been carrying it with him for two weeks, since the last griefquake that left him a shattered mess, collapsed in his driveway staring in a traumatized daze at the autumn light sifting through the leaves, reminding him of those weeks after Damon's death.

On that day, he'd gone in the house after picking himself up, and he'd passed out on the sofa, exhausted and wrung out from his emotions, for almost four hours. After a shower, and a cold glass of water, Cole decided to try his day again. He'd opened the door, ready to head into the office better late than never. There, in the center of the mat—placed perfectly in the middle and facing the door like a valentine or a message—lay the rock. It could have come from anywhere. Perhaps he kicked it up from the drive on his stumble into the house. Maybe a neighbor had dropped it. Or Emily. Or a stranger.

Cole still doesn't know, but he now claims it for his own. He keeps it in his coat pocket, his talisman, his hardest heart, his beautiful rock of a heart. He runs his fingers over it when he wants to think of Damon and stay tethered to the earth.

As the sounds of the night surround him, he walks, the rush of cars on the road push the boundaries of his own fear with proximity. He fingers the stone and remembers. Soft hair that he loved to cup with his hand as they kissed. Sweet tongue that had sometimes tasted of coffee and other times of beer.

"I love you. Don't forget it." Cool fingers, tender on his cheek.

The timbre of Damon's voice, the way he said, "Cole."

The strong muscles of his back beneath Cole's palms.

Each commanding thing he ever heard Damon say. The patience and respect he had for Cole's boundaries. All of these things and more turn over in Cole's mind, polished like mirrors, peered at, breathed on, and searched endlessly for more detail. His fingers run over the stone in his pocket, holding him together.

"I miss you," Cole says aloud. "So much."

A noise from behind, somewhere in the woods behind the house to his left, grabs his attention, and he sees a shadow move. A deer, no doubt. Or a dog. Perhaps a bobcat. Cole smiles at that thought, though he knows he shouldn't. As a small child, he saw a bobcat in the woods near their house, and his father had kept the children from wandering after dark until the bobcat's carcass was found, slaughtered by no one knew who. Ever since, Cole has entertained fantasies of meeting a bobcat up close again, finding the idea of its teeth tearing into him not nearly as terrifying as he should.

His mind shifts again, going to the past, and he thinks of the day he met Damon. The way his flesh had sung as though a chord vibrated inside him the moment Damon's eyes met his from across the room at Emily and Alex's Halloween party. He'd taken Cole's breath away with his curly strawberry-blond hair, piercing green eyes, and sharp, narrow jaw. He'd worn a white lab coat over his jeans and polo shirt, so Cole had asked him, pulse overload in his ears, if he was dressed up as a doctor.

"I am a doctor," Damon had said. Then he pointed to a Hello, My Name Is… nametag pinned to his lapel.

"Your name is God?" Cole had laughed. "Really?"

"That's what the men I've been with yell out during sex. I thought it an appropriate costume." He'd given Cole a long up and down glance. "My real name's Damon. What's yours?"

Cole still remembers the way his face had flushed hot, and his palms had gone sweaty. He still remembers the zing in his nether regions, unexpected and unusual, and the way he'd gone breathless and tongued tied under Damon's hot gaze. Immediate attraction was strange for him, unusual and scary, and he'd almost put on the brakes so hard that, if it hadn't been for Emily and Alex's timely intervention, he might have ruined it all before it even had a chance to begin.

They'd arrived at Damon's elbows, both of them shining with excited smiles, and they'd guided them into a conversation that softened Cole's resistance and fear. Damon was a pediatrician specializing in pediatric oncology, and the way his voice gentled when he spoke of his work made Cole's insides shake like Jell-O.

Once Emily and Alex went on their way to greet the rest of their friends, Damon had led Cole outside to escape the stuffy house, and they'd sat by Emily's apartment pool, talking and laughing all night. Their interests had intersected at nearly every point, and where they didn't, Damon's respectful treatment of Cole's opinion was shiver-inducingly sexy.

Cole knows now that he should have slept with him that first night. But his reticence, self-consciousness, and virginity had plagued him and kept him from expressing his love in the most intimate of physical ways. He'd always thought there would be time to explore all of that together. Time for him to get fit and get past his fear that he couldn't ever live up to the other men Damon had been with, the ones with experience and skill. The men Damon hadn't had to work so hard to get.

Cole huffs. He was a fool. Death doesn't wait for men to grow courage to live their life. Death just acts without remorse or care. It takes and devours.

The cars are speeding, going much too fast for the road they're on, well over the speed limit. Cole shakes his fist at one, even, though it's mostly for his own entertainment. They can't see him at all in his dark coat and dark pants.

Walking at night might not be the brightest idea, Cole thinks, but if he can't drink himself to death, and he can't play with sharp knives, or overdose on pills because it's too active of an attempt to do something he's not even sure he wants to do, then this nonsense, this silly walk at night on a road never intended for pedestrian travel, is just the thing to tempt fate. He can feel Damon coming closer and closer to him with every car that whizzes by, and he clenches his jaw, spreads his arms wide, and dares a car to hit him, dares the speeding vehicles to swerve a little to their right, and take him out of this world.

He's on the edge of a ravine now. There's no room for error between the cars going by and the ditch below. It's like standing on the very edge of a cliff, throwing things over the side to watch them hit bottom, thinking, if only momentarily, of what Damon must have felt when Alex lost control of the car, how frightened he must have been as it went over the side of the bridge, when he lay dying. The moments when he knew it was too late.

Cole's stomach lurches as a car does swerve, and his eyes go wide in the glare of the headlights. A thud against his back throws him forward and then rolls him to the side. He falls down, pitching over hard rocks and sharp sticks. His head hits hard as he skids to the bottom of the ditch. The dead weight on his back is person-shaped and strong. Panic rockets through him, and he tries to get to his knees.

"Don't move. You may have broken something," his

attacker commands.

The voice feels like his dreams. It slips into him and twines through him, up his spine, and around his ribs, and clenches at his heart.

Cole moves, and his ribs ache, but it's pitch black out, not a star in the sky, no moon to light the darkness, and he can't see. The person next to him—it is a person—is nothing but breath on his cheek, and hands on his body, feeling him, touching him in search of blood or a bent limb, and Cole turns inside out, because that voice, that voice, *that voice.*

"Talk to me," Cole says, grabbing at the figure, clenching on wiry, muscular arms, and holding tight, too hard.

"Cole, hold still."

Cole lets go and lurches away, scooting over the earth, gravel and stones digging into his hands and ass as he moves back fast. "Who are you?"

Something slides down his face, and he reaches up— it's wet, and there's a lot of it. His fingers slip through the blood.

"You're hurt. Where's your phone? You need to call for an ambulance."

"Who are you?" Cole says again. He doesn't need an ambulance. He's twenty-four years old and he's survived more than most people his age. Inside, he's forty if he's a day, and yet he's got years left to go. Years. Head wound or no. If he's going to die tonight, it's the cars that will do him in, and this person, this voice, this terrifying man next to him who hasn't let that happen. Not tonight.

The shadow beside him moves forward and Cole braces himself. Hands ransack his pockets, and Cole says, "I'll give you money, if that's what you want."

He feels strange now. He doesn't understand why he's here. His head is hurting, and he blinks hard, because something is off, something is wrong, and this man, this person, this voice that sounds exactly like Damon is leaning him down to the ground and pulling Cole's cell phone from his pocket.

The light from the phone illuminates the man's face, and Cole shakes his head. "No," Cole says. "I don't believe it. It can't be you."

Darkness and a dream voice asking for an ambulance penetrate his mind, and then nothing else.

CHAPTER 2

"A CONCUSSION," HIS older sister, Rosanna, says. "Really, Cole, what were you thinking?"

Cole shakes his head and says nothing, because what is there to say? Besides, he wants to leave this horrible place as soon as possible.

The hospital is hard for him on the best of days. Right now, it's crawling with painful memories, and being in the room where Damon… Being in the room where he died isn't helping. It seemed like some kind of cruel fate that this is the room they assigned him after the ambulance brought him in. He almost told them he couldn't go in there, but he tried to convince himself that it's a room like any other, and fourteen hours later, he's still telling himself the same thing.

He let them check him over completely, not getting any sleep at all, spending the whole time remembering every second of those last moments with Damon, playing them over and over in his mind. It's only been an hour, though, since he's allowed them to call his sister.

Rosanna comes closer, takes his chin in her hand,

and says, "Cole, were you trying to hurt yourself?"

Cole bats her hand away, frustrated. "No! No, of course not."

It feels like an insult that she asks, especially when it's been so hard, when he fights the dark thoughts so desperately; he can't cope with the idea that depression might win. That she thinks it maybe already has. Never mind that some days it's a close thing. Never mind that it was a close thing tonight, even. He needs her unconditional belief in him.

"Then what were you doing? Walking alone on the side of that busy, narrow road? It sure seems like you were trying to get yourself killed."

Cole shakes his head and looks away. He can't meet her eyes right now, not with all of this confusion flooding through him, the shame of what he does when no one is watching, the way he tempts almost anything to take him out because he can't do it himself. Because Damon would never want him to do it.

"I was just…walking." He hears his own voice, knows how broken it sounds, and he closes his eyes as he swallows. To explain this would be to explain how very not okay he is, and has been, and probably always will be, and his sister doesn't need to hear that. She knows already anyway. She probably feels it in her bones. But he can't tell her. He doesn't want to be the one who puts that look on her face. Not today. He doesn't have the room to deal with her pain, too.

Rosanna clutches him to her, holding him in a tight hug of perfume and the warm scent of her skin that smells like home. It's the smell of comfort from skinned knees when they were kids, which later became the confusion and pain of her rejection when he came out, and the joy of her acceptance after time soothed her shock, and the honest wounding of being two very different humans in the same family. It's a scent mixed of pain and love, and he takes it in, finding it not at all stable, not at all four walls and a roof, but something more primal and familiar to him—the scent of the family that shaped of his body and soul.

"Come on," Rosanna says, touching his cheek. "Let me take you home."

Cole nods and climbs out of the hospital bed. As he pulls on his coat to go, he thrusts his hand into the pocket. Not there. It's not there. The other pocket is empty, too. Rushing blood roars in his ears, and he grips the table to keep standing. The heart, his talisman, must have fallen out when he tumbled into the ditch, or…was it…did he… The person who called the ambulance? Did he take it? His hands were in Cole's pockets. He sounded like Damon…but it isn't, and it can't be. Cole is losing his mind. Concussed. He's concussed. But there's no doubt about it. The rock is gone.

"Cole?" Rosanna asks, concern in her voice. "Should I call a doctor? Are you going to pass out?"

Cole isn't going to pass out. No, he's going to crack,

completely crack, because he *needs* that rock. He needs it because it's real and it's what lets him be okay when he thinks of Damon. It works better than anything else ever has.

"I'll call the—"

"No," Cole says, raising a hand to his mouth, holding back the tears. "It's just this room," he says. "It was in this room."

Rosanna is clearly confused, but when she looks around, a realization comes over her face. "Jesus Christ, you should have said something." She grips Cole's arm and says, "Let's get you out of here."

His house isn't a comfort to him, though, and he starts to pack his bag. He has to get out of town, go somewhere else. He needs to head up the mountain. Just for a few days until his head is screwed on again.

Rosanna watches with her arms folded over her chest.

"Just be sure to tell Dad about what the doctor told you. No sleeping for six hours. And he needs to wake you in the night."

Cole manages to shake himself free of his panic long enough to smile at her, tilt his head in some version of amusement and say, "Yes, warden. I can handle it."

"Okay," she says, but she sounds doubtful. "I'll...just call him."

Cole doesn't argue. He doesn't care. She can call his dad and talk to him for ten hours about this mess, and it won't change that Cole is clearly out of his mind, and the only thing he wants more than a life that went entirely different one September day two years ago is just to get up to his father's cabin, sleep with the windows open, and hike up to the waterfall for a while to clear his head.

"I'll drive you," she says. "You can't be driving anyway."

It isn't what Cole wants to hear. If she goes, then she'll stay and start a fight with their dad. Things will be *difficult*, and it'll become about so much more than what Cole needs right now.

"I'll call Emily to come get me," Cole says.

It's the better side of the equation, even if it'll take twice as long to get to his final destination. The idea of Rosanna and his dad together, the force of them, how they've always fought with their claws out ever since their parents' divorce. Rosanna blamed Dad for their mother's broken heart, unhealed even on her deathbed, and she'll never let that go. He can't handle all that history. He just wants to escape it for now.

His best friend Emily will just look at him with worried eyes and ask incredibly unhelpful questions, but she'll end it all with a hug and she'll tell him she loves him. It'll make it just that much easier to keep on breathing, to keep on living. He does it for them, after all. For them and for Damon.

Damn him.

No! Cole thinks. He takes that last bit back. It still

terrifies him to be angry with Damon, like that will somehow be the thing that drives all the memories away, that it'll make Damon dead forever and truly. Cole sits down on the bed and rests his head in his hands.

Damon is dead. It's neither here nor there what Cole thinks or says or believes. It changes nothing.

Sometimes Cole knows it's ridiculous that he's been grieving for Damon so much longer than he even knew him. But there's comfort to be had in the memories of the times they shared. It's the regrets over what he never got that hurt him the most.

"I called Emily," Rosanna's voice cuts into his thoughts.

Cole is grateful. He doesn't have the energy now to explain why he needs to get to the cabin, or why he doesn't want Rosanna there, too. He's grateful that, for whatever reason, his sister has arranged for him to get what he needs without him having to fight for it.

"Thank you," he says, and he sits. And he waits.

"ROSANNA SAYS THAT you might have been trying to kill yourself," Emily says.

She's gripping the wheel with both hands, one at the two and one at the ten, just the way their high school driving instructor taught them both. Her knuckles are white. But she's looking at him instead of the road.

Cole waves a hand dismissively. "No. I wouldn't do that."

That's mostly true.

"Are you sure?" Emily asks. "Because I don't think I could handle it—"

"You won't have to handle it, Emily," Cole says, and he looks right at her so that she can see how serious he is. They've been friends since sixth grade when he came out to her about his crush on bucktoothed Joey Taylor. "I wouldn't…I don't even want…" He sighs. This part is harder. It's a little less true. "I wish Rosanna hadn't said that to you. I don't want to die."

"So, what happened out there?" Emily asks. "Really?"

"I don't know. I don't want to talk about it."

She gives him one of her exasperated faces. He's so familiar with every variation of that expression from years of being her friend.

Even though she respects how much he's grieved for Damon, he also knows she thinks he's let this pain go too deep and last too long. He knows she wishes she could tell him something like, "Get up! Get over it! Go out with a hot guy! Kiss him! Do whatever it is you didn't do with Damon and tear the Band-Aid off! You only knew him for a year and a few months, for heaven's sake. Get over it."

She's as patient as a saint to never say those things, Cole thinks. More patient than he might be if the roles were reversed.

Cole watches the trees flash by the windows of the moving car, and they're coming up to the corner where it happened. "Emily, pull over."

"Why?" she asks.

"Just pull the car over," he says, and he starts to open the door, which seems to scare her. So she does as he says, jerking off the road a bit and almost ending up in the ditch.

"What are you doing?" she yells, as he climbs out of the car and jogs across the road.

He hears her car door slam and knows she's following, but he doesn't wait for her to catch up. He skids down into the ditch, slipping and sliding along the steep bank, until he reaches the bottom.

The night before, he was carried up the embankment on a stretcher, alone, and the EMTs had sworn there was no one there when they arrived. But Cole's mind supplies him with something different: memories of hands, a voice, and the scent of something familiar and gone too long. Something he'd barely known before it was taken from his life. Fragile, fleeting, and Cole finds himself sniffing the air for it now, like a dog, like an animal hunting his way home.

"Cole!" Emily calls from above.

"Don't come down here!" Cole calls back. "I just…I think I lost something here. I need to—I need to look. Just give me a minute."

Emily stands with her arms crossed over her chest, her hip thrust out in annoyance.

He turns back to the ground around him. It's disturbed all over, the marks of the EMTs shoes, the scuffs from where the rocks were knocked loose and tumbled, down, and Cole gets on his hands and knees, pawing through the earth looking for it, running his fingers over the sharp edges of rocks that aren't the one he's trying to find.

There's the sound of more falling rock, and Cole glances up to see Emily skidding down the side of the embankment.

"Fine," she says. "Let me help. What are you looking for?"

Cole swallows. He doesn't want to say. "Just…this…thing. It's important to me. It's just…"

"Um, a little more information, please," Emily says, rolling her eyes at him.

"Never mind," Cole says, standing up. "It's not here. I don't know. Let's go."

Emily throws her hands up. "Are you kidding me? I messed up my new manicure to help you!" She waves toward the ground. "Come on, let's look some more."

"No," Cole says, starting up the embankment, slowly, having to use his hands to climb and getting them filthy with dirt. "It's not here."

"What's not here?" Emily insists.

Cole ignores her.

Riding toward the cabin, Cole studies his nails. There's dirt caked under them, and his hands are grubby. A grave digger, he thinks. And he doesn't know why. But it's true. He's filthy like he's been out digging graves, and he tilts his head back against the head rest, as exhaustion overwhelms him.

"Don't sleep," Emily says. "Just rest, but don't sleep."

Her voice is gentle, and Cole knows what a bad sign that is. That means she believes he's really gone around the bend again. And it's true that he's not supposed to sleep, but he closes his eyes and lets it claim him.

If he dies, Damon won't meet him at the gates of heaven to tell him it counts as suicide, will he? He won't accuse him of killing himself, will he? And even if he does, Damon will still welcome him into his arms, right?

He sleeps until the car stops and he's at his father's house.

THE WATERFALL IS restorative. He sits by the edge, watching the roaring slash of the water, feeling the mist against his face. The birds land in the trees around him and then take flight, black, undulating waves of them headed south.

At first, he does what he used to do to get by. He thinks of nothing. He makes himself focus on the blades of golden autumn grass, and he concentrates on making sure that he doesn't allow any threat of thought to run through him. Observation, he can handle. Thinking often hurts too much.

Finally, as he feels his body acclimate, adjusts down from the heightened state that he's been in since the prior night, and he lets himself turn his mind onto the subject itself.

There is a man. Or he believes there is. A man who pushed him out the path of the car. A man who sounds like Damon, and smells like Damon, and—*no, I don't believe you*—looks like Damon.

"Damon is dead," Cole says aloud. He's said it before, and he'll say it again. "Damon is dead." The water spills from the height of the waterfall, and he rubs his eyes with his fingers. "You imagined it," he says.

The emotionless sky stares down at him without comment. The pine trees shuffle in the breeze, their needles rubbing out strange, whispered disagreement. A crow screams from across the mountain.

"Who called the ambulance, then?" he asks, and the crow caws again.

"Who're you talking to, son?"

Cole stiffens, before turning to face his father, the autumn sun backlighting him through the canopy of trees, so that his father is a shadow of blue jeans and a flannel shirt emerging from the trail.

"Myself," Cole says, and turns back to the waterfall.

Dad is warm from the walk as he sits on the rock next to Cole, and their shoulders touch. Cole leans into him. He smells his dad's sweat, and the scent of musty books, and he smiles, because *this* is four walls and a roof, even if the door is always open and people are always flowing in and out.

Though Cole knows that his dad's open-door policy with women caused the problems in his parents' marriage, he's always felt like safety to Cole. He's always protected Cole and let him be who he needs to be. When he came out, his dad just said, "Okay, son. Thanks for telling me."

And that was that.

"Rosanna called to tell me that you told the EMTs some pretty wild things last night," Dad says, plucking a piece of dry grass, and twiddling it his fingers.

"Oh, yeah?" Cole says.

"Yeah. Something about Damon being there."

Cole nods, his lips already twisting to hold back the tears.

"Son, I know things have been—difficult is an understatement. But I need you to be honest with me now. Right here. Just the two of us. Have you been thinking of hurting yourself? Are you feeling suicidal?"

Cole can't stop the tears, and he lets out a puff of air and shakes his head. He's only just gotten himself back together, and a few sentences from his dad have him blown apart again. "No," he says.

"Cole," Dad says, gently. "What happened? You were doing so much better lately. What's caused this setback?"

Cole can't seem to answer that question. Doing so much better is relative. He's been through cycles before where he feels like he's able to ignore the hole in his life, and he moves ahead, and everyone around him breathes a sigh of relief. *This is it*, he can feel them thinking. *This is when Cole finally gets it together, and we can all move on from this terrible tragedy, and Cole will be happy again.* He hates feeling like he's letting them down.

"Nothing," Cole says. "I was fine. I mean, I am fine."

Dad sighs. "Son, you're not fine."

"I know," Cole agrees. "I'll try to do better."

"It's not about doing better, Cole. Listen—you do everything just fine."

Cole shrugs. A flock of crows goes up in a chatter of noise. He watches them swirl in the sky, before pointing their beaks toward warmer weather.

"Tell me what happened last night," Dad says, clearly trying to take another tack, to come at this from another side. The most important side. The one that is relevant.

"I was walking home from Southern Grace," Cole says, and he can feel his dad holding back from making a comment on the intelligence of that particular exercise. "It was dark; the cars probably couldn't see me well. I don't know." Oh, he knows. He knows so well what he was risking. "A car swerved. Someone pushed me down, and I fell into the ditch." Cole touches the bandage on his forehead. "Hit my head. I remember saying that I didn't need an ambulance."

Where's your phone? You need to call for an ambulance.

"The man who pushed me. He…sounded like Damon. He *looked* like Damon." Cole says.

"It was dark," Dad says. "There was probably just a resemblance. And you saw what you wanted to see."

Cole picks up a stone from the ground beside him and throws it into the water swirling beneath the falls, anger ripping through him. "Why would I want to see that?" he demands.

"You loved him," Dad says. "You still grieve for him. Part of you will always want to see him."

"Stop," Cole says, his chest aching so much that he feels like he will break if the sobs he's holding in start to come up.

Dad puts his arm around Cole's shoulder, and when he draws Cole to him, Cole starts to shake. It's been a long time since it's been this bad, so much sadness that he can't at least pretend in front of other people, so much that he dissolves into the pain heedless of a witness.

There's no choice. He lets his father hold him as he cries.

✕

CLIMBING THE STAIRS to the guest room in his dad's mountain cabin that night, Cole is worn through. He feels translucent in his exhaustion. All he can think of is getting into bed, and he prays he won't dream. The door to his room is half open, and he frowns. He usually leaves it closed, if only to discourage his father's three cats from getting in. And there they are in the middle of this bed, cute and sweet but shedding onto the comforter. Cole's highly allergic to their fur. He tries not to be annoyed.

He peels his clothes off and pulls a soft pair of sweats and an old X-Men T-shirt from the dresser drawer. He runs his hand over the front of it, remembering when his dad gave it to him as a surprise gift one day, "Just for being you." Cole smiles. His father gets him.

Cole turns to the bed to change the sheets and feels his blood run cold.

There, on his pillow, is the rock. Heart-shaped. The exact one that had been in his pocket. Cole approaches it like it's a bomb, and he sees that beneath the rock is a piece of paper. A note. In tiny, perfect letters. Written in black ink.

Cole picks up the rock, clenches it in his fist. He takes the paper between his thumb and forefinger.

This belongs to you.

Cole sits on his bed and stares at the wall. His blood is roaring in his ears, and his heart is thumping wildly in his chest. He says softly, "No. This belongs to you."

"Sheriff Hunt," Cole says, standing in front of her desk, his hands stuffed into his pants pockets and with what he hopes is a sweet grin on his face. He knows that Sheriff Tanya Hunt goes a little soft for that smile. He used to flash it at her back when she was his babysitter many years ago. "I know it's unusual, but it would really help me to…understand."

Sheriff Hunt doesn't want to let him hear the tape. He can see that clearly. But he has to listen for himself.

"Cole," she says. "I don't know what to tell you. Normally, I wouldn't hesitate. I just don't want you fooling yourself, honey."

The Maryville police station is bustling, and Cole has to move aside as they drag a guy past in handcuffs. Sheriff Hunt rolls her eyes at the guy and says, "I'll see *you* later. I'll be hoping for more cooperation next time."

Cole smiles, close mouthed, and then says, "I'm not fooling myself. So, the recording?"

"Cole…" she says, and gives him her patented discouraging look.

Cole doesn't have time to wonder who has told Sheriff Hunt about his ravings to the EMTs. Maryville is a small town. People know each other, especially the longtime locals. Word spreads quickly. What he needs to do now is convince her that he's not insane, and that he has the right to hear the recording. It's public record, after all. She can't actually deny him.

"Sheriff Hunt," he says, smiling and shaking his head. "You don't need to worry. I had a concussion. I was confused. I just want to hear the recording so that I can…see if there's any information that can help me track down the guy. I want to thank him."

Sheriff Hunt gives him the look that means she knows he's full of shit, and she says, "I don't think he wants to be thanked. Or he would have stuck around. Call it a good citizen doing a good deed. Some people don't want the attention."

"Exactly. That doesn't mean that I don't have a right to investigate my rescuer. Or at least attempt to thank him, anyway."

Sheriff Hunt's phone rings and she picks it up, turning her back to him. Whatever the call is about, it's clear that Sheriff Hunt has no more time for him, and she waves over an officer who's wandering past her desk.

Putting her hand over the mouthpiece of the phone, Sheriff Hunt says, "Get Cole Hart here what he wants."

Cole grins and gives Sheriff Hunt a thumbs up. "Thank you!" he mouths.

She narrows her eyes and says, "Don't make me regret this," before turning back to her call.

An hour later, Cole has listened to the call fifty times. He's sweaty, and shivering, and the officer has checked on him twice, asking if he's okay.

"Sure. Of course," he says. "Can I get a copy of

this?"

The officer shrugs. "Chief said whatever you want. So, whatever you want."

"I want a copy." He thrusts a thumbnail drive at the guy who reluctantly takes it.

"All right. I'll just get this to Erica. She does that sort of thing."

Cole nods and watches him leave the room. He can tell the guy thinks he's off. He doesn't care. He clicks play again.

Yeah, I need an ambulance on Highway 10 close to the mile marker. Left side ditch if you're headed east. Head injury. No neck trauma. He's out cold.

Cole thinks that once he has his thumbnail drive back in his hand he should go to Maryville Billiards, order a drink, and then another, because he knows that voice, hears it in his dreams at night, hears it when he's trying not to fall into a panic; he knows it anywhere, anytime, always.

Instead, Cole drives back to the scene. He pulls over and stands at the side of the ditch. He gazes down at the darkness at the bottom and he says, "I saw you die. I *know* they put your heart in him. They burned your body. I helped spread the ashes."

The sun screams down around him, bright and strong, cutting through the air and illuminating the dirt and rocks below.

He bites his lip. "Am I going crazy?"

Cole waits. He listens. There's nothing. Not a ghost of a wind, just freezing cold air that burns his nose and eyes.

It's been a few days now since he's been into his office for work. He knows Michael is waiting on his approval on a few important items for Appalachian Rainbows, and he should take care of that. He shouldn't be standing on the side of the road talking to ghosts. Ghosts that have voices that are real enough to be recorded and hands that touch. Cole can still feel how gentle those hands were with him.

He gets into his car, starts the engine, and knows he should go to his office. He takes out his phone instead and calls Emily.

"I DON'T THINK I have anything like that," Emily says, bending over the tiny box of Damon's stuff that she's kept for Alex in case he ever returns. They were cousins, but more than that, they'd been best friends. Everything else, the important stuff Alex had kept of Damon's after his parents took what they wanted, she's already given to Cole.

"Just…a note, or…something he wrote," Cole says.

Emily sighs, tucks her hair behind her ears, and says, "No—but, you know, if it's that important to you, then you can try the hospital. Some of personnel files? They should have them still in storage, don't you think? Surely you could convince someone there to show you *something*."

There are so many things about Emily that Cole appreciates. Right now, though, Cole appreciates that Emily doesn't even ask *why* Cole needs to see some of Damon's handwriting. Nor does she suggest he make contact with Damon's homophobic family. She's too smart for that.

Even if Emily's made it clear on more than one occasion that she thinks Cole should put the past aside and move on, at least more than he has, she never suggests that he's wrong to have a sudden need to re-read Damon's old texts, or to want to see his handwriting, because Emily *knows* that's part of losing someone. It's the desire to prove that, yes, this person truly existed; their fingers pressed the pen against this paper and wrote these very words.

Alex might not have died, but Emily grieves him all the same.

"Thanks, Emily," Cole says, hugging her and letting her cling.

"Another rough day?" she asks.

"You know how it is," he says.

"I do." She sighs. "It comes and it goes."

Cole takes a few minutes then to act less insane, to focus on Emily, and he asks, "Did you tell him? Michael, I mean? Did you tell him yes? Like you said you would the other day at Southern Grace?"

She smiles and it's beautiful. "I did. We have a date. Tonight."

Cole's answering smile is genuine, and he hugs her again. "I'm glad, Emily. I'm happy for you."

He can see her standing in the doorway of her house as he climbs into his car and drives away. Another thing Emily hasn't asked is whether he's been cleared for driving yet. He has not. So he's glad she doesn't.

Despite it being a very good idea, the hospital isn't that interested, though, in giving him access to any personnel records simply because Cole wants to see his long-dead boyfriend's handwriting one more time.

Hannah, an old friend of Damon's who still works in HR, is stalling on him, citing protocol, and Cole's seconds away from doing the unthinkable and breaking down right there, when Maris, Damon's favorite nurse says, "Mr. Hart? I'm sorry, I couldn't help but overhear, and I have…something? Maybe?"

She sounds so uncertain that Cole feels a sudden empathy for the woman. She had cared for Damon, too.

"You have something?" Cole asks, narrowing his eyes and staring at her. "What do you mean?"

Maris looks at the floor and then back up at Cole. "When…when Dr. Black…died. I cleared out his desk and locker for you. Do you remember?"

Of course Cole remembers. He has the box in his closet at home. He'd been so grateful Maris had given the effects to him instead of Damen's parents—who hadn't even thought to ask for them. Cole sorts through the box now and again, though he shouldn't. For the same reason that he's supposedly here now. Just to remember. To feel close.

"Well, there was a piece of paper, and it had…a list?" Maris says it like it's a question. "Like a grocery list. And I don't know why, but I kept it?"

"You kept it?" Cole asks, and he feels like shaking her, because that paper should have been his. He should have been able to touch it, and kiss it, and damn it, she's had it for two years? Why?

"Yes," Maris says. "I, uh…I kept it because I felt so guilty? For not being able to help him on the day he died?"

Cole clenches his jaw, crosses his arms over his chest and hopes he doesn't look as enraged as he feels. He's hot and cold, and he feels violated that she's kept this grocery list from him. He knows how ridiculous that is, how only three days ago, he would have told her that he was glad that Maris wanted to remember Damon and that nothing had been her fault. At the moment, though, he only feels like this list should have been his all along.

"It's in my purse," Maris says. "I keep it there to remind myself that people we care about can be gone just like that. And that sometimes, even when that person is hard on you? Or your feelings? You should remember that they…love people. And buy sandwich meat."

Cole blinks because somewhere during that comment, his rage swings into tears, and he's got to keep them back. "Damon was a fan of a meaty sandwich," he says, biting at his lip.

"Do you want me to get it?" Maris asks.

Cole fights to keep his composure but nods, and he feels Hannah's hand on his shoulder as Maris walks away, head down, her soft shoes silent on the floor.

"Cole," Hannah says, softly. "Can I recommend that you to talk to someone?"

He's had this conversation with her before. A year ago, when she'd run into him at the grocery store and he'd started to cry remembering Damon. Now, he shakes his head, and manages a smile. "Hannah, I'm okay. Really. I just don't want to forget him."

Hannah's eyes are gentle as she says, "You'll never forget him, Cole."

"I know," Cole says, finally mastering his emotions. "I really do know that, Hannah."

"It's been two years," she says.

"I know," Cole says again.

She clucks quietly and then sees Maris approaching. "All right, then," she says. "Let me know if you change your mind. I keep notes on LGBT-friendly therapists. I'm happy to provide names to you."

The grocery list is on the back of a receipt. Cole glances at the items purchased, and his eyes go wide to see the abbreviations TROJA and ASTRO that speak of plans that he and Damon had never been able to implement. He wonders if Maris ever noticed, but he doubts it. She seems innocent as she points out, "It's just a few things he wrote down. I shouldn't have kept it."

Cole takes a moment to make her feel okay, to let her know he's not angry anymore, and then he leaves with the note in his hand, afraid to look at the words until he's alone.

CHAPTER 3

Ham
Salami
American
Swiss
Bologne
Trash bags

The words are clearly rushed, written by a fast hand, in a hurry, and Cole can imagine Damon sitting at his desk, jotting it down on the back of the receipt, and then heading out to see his young patients before meeting up with Alex at The Book and Bird for dinner.

Cole looks at the date on the receipt, printed in light purple above the purchases, and he swallows. Two days before. Just two days before he died, Damon bought what they would have needed to make love. Things that they never got to—

Cole shakes his head. He needs to focus. That's pointless to think of now. He needs to not get caught up in regrets, because what's important is whether or not the writing—

Except it isn't possible. Cole saw Damon die. But he has to know if it's the same, if somehow the writing on the note from the cabin is Damon's.

Back in the office, Cole locks the door behind him and leans against it for a moment taking slow breaths, before rubbing his forehead with his hand. The bruise aches, and he presses it on purpose, trying to feel it, to know that he's not dreaming. He doesn't even know what he's doing, or why. This thing—this idea that's rooted in his mind—it's impossible, and maybe Hannah is right. Maybe he should talk to someone.

Cole swallows, closes his eyes, and thinks of the night on the busy road, the thud of the body pushing him out of the way. *Cole, hold still.* He said 'Cole.' He knew exactly who it was he was pushing out of the path of the car. And his eyes, when Cole saw them in the glow of the phone, they were exactly the same.

Cole moves to his desk and sits down, takes another deep breath, and puts the palms of his hands down flat on the surface and gathers the courage. He takes the note from his wallet, unfolds it carefully, his fingers trembling, and he places the paper next to the list Damon had written out sometime in the two days before he died.

The list is hurried. The note is precise, solid, as though each letter was considered fully and drawn with distinct purpose. Cole studies them, side by side. He's no graphologist, but the letters appear to be made in similar ways. The tail of the Gs are comparable, the vowels created in the same way, and Cole thinks that if the list had been written in the same meticulous manner, the handwriting would look like that of the note.

But it's madness.

He shakes his head and steeples his hands in front of his mouth. The man by the side of the road—Cole goes over the moment again in his mind. It was dark, pitch black, he was shocked, and he'd hit his head, he can't begin to be certain that what he'd seen was not just the product of his concussion.

And the stone heart on his pillow? The note? The most likely explanation is incredibly unpleasant to consider—the man who rescued him is now stalking him. Perhaps was stalking him even that night.

Cole crosses his arms on the desk and rests his head against them. He wants to cry. He wants to feel sad now that he's come back to reality. Instead, he's just hollow and tired, like the crazed grief and hope and frantic investigation of the last day is all that he's made of, and now that it's gone, he's depleted, a shell.

He sits at his desk until the day has completely passed into night. He sits in the glare of the overhead lights and stares at the letters on the note, the letters on the receipt, and he spins the stone heart around on the desk, the clatter of it against the wood real and annoying. Cole runs his fingers over the surface, puts it into his pocket, and stands to leave.

First, he places the note and the receipt inside a book he keeps in the drawer of his desk. It's a bound version of the Hardiest Hearts' annual report, and he smooths the note and the receipt flat against page 19 before closing them there.

As he walks into the cold, autumn night air, he fondles the rock in his pocket. He's almost to his car when Michael Saint John exits the building behind him.

"Boss!" he yells, laughing. "Wait up!"

Cole turns around and watches the tall, lanky man walk toward him. In the darkness, he looks about Damon's height, and Cole rubs his fingers over his eyes, thinking, *See? A lot of people can look like Damon in the dark.*

He imagines that a lot of people might *feel* like Damon in the dark, too. Skin on skin. But he's never been able to bring himself to act on his sexual needs that way, even though he's considered it more than once. *You don't truly know how Damon would have felt in the dark, and you'll never know,* his mind helpfully supplies, so he's twisted up inside, aching, and frustrated when Michael catches him.

"Hey, kid," Michael says. It's a joke between them. Michael, eight years older than Cole, calls him "boss," or "kid," and sometimes "boss kid," and for some reason it always makes them both laugh. But Cole doesn't laugh tonight. "You're here late."

"You, too," Cole says. "What's up?"

"All of that responsibility that you shuffled onto me today. Made me miss my date with Emily."

Cole groans. "No, tell me you didn't cancel."

"Postponed," Michael says.

"I'm sorry," Cole says. "I didn't even think that—"

"Why should you?" Michael says. "I'm your employee, not your friend. And, besides, I'm glad you trust me enough to take over when you need the help. I was happy to do it."

Cole reaches out to shake Michael's hand, and starts to say something about being glad he can trust Michael, too, when Michael grabs his hand and pulls him into a hug.

"You hang in there, boss kid," Michael says. "I don't know exactly what's going on with you right now. But you've got my full support."

Cole pats Michael's back, allows himself to be held for a moment longer, and then Michael lets him go.

"So, I guess I might be a little bit your friend, after all," Michael says, gripping his arm. "I worry about you, Cole. You take a lot on yourself, and Emily says lately you've been exhibiting... Well, we want you to be around for a long time. That's all."

Cole crosses his arms over his chest and smiles. He's pleased, if confused, by this turn of events. He likes Michael, and he wishes that they were closer. Sometimes he misses having close friends. He's got Emily, and he has his sister and his father, but after Damon died—well, making and keeping friends always seems so fraught.

"Thanks, Michael," Cole says. "I'll be okay. I'm

just…" He shrugs.

"Remembering," Michael fills in.

"Yeah." Cole nods.

"I don't know if you're aware, but I lost my wife in a skiing accident," Michael says. "It's sudden and it's senseless. I understand."

Cole has heard this through the grapevine, but Michael's never mentioned it to him directly before. Michael doesn't seem to be as messed up about his loss as Cole is over Damon, and he wonders how Michael healed so well. Probably because Michael has plenty of memories to indulge in, and not just lists and lists of regrets.

"How long ago?" Cole asks.

"Going on six years," Michael says. "And it's just like I told Emily—some days are harder than others. One day, I'm fine. And the next I'm having a hard time making it through. It gets easier and easier, though, to have those days when you remember the person you lost without letting it tear you apart."

Cole's heard this a dozen times, from so many people, and the only problem is that he doesn't want to get to a place where losing Damon doesn't tear him apart. In fact, he's terrified of that day. On that day, he's let Damon be truly dead.

Cole catches his breath at that thought, and his hand comes up to his mouth.

"You okay?" Michael asks again.

Cole nods. "Fine. Good. I need to get going, though."

Michael smiles again, and says, "Sure thing, boss. I'm going to stop by Emily's and see if I can get a late start on the date."

"Good plan," Cole says.

"Chin up," Michael says. "We have important work to do. Keep that in mind."

"I always do."

"I know," Michael agrees. "I find that completely impressive about you. How you really want to do something good with the insurance money he left you. I'm proud to work for you."

Cole laughed softly, shaking his head. "You don't need to flatter me. You've got the job."

Michael shakes him gently by the shoulder. "I'm only telling you this because I don't have to. See you tomorrow. I have a lady to beg forgiveness."

Cole watches Michael cross the parking lot to climb into his car and waits until he's pulling out of the lot to get into his own. He locks the doors and stares out into the dark around him. The edge of the parking lot is bordered with woods, and his eyes are drawn to a movement in the darkness there. Squinting, he thinks it's a person. He stares, trying to make out more, but the shadow doesn't move, and there's no way that anyone could be that still.

Cole turns the engine over, and flips on the headlights. The beam hits a man standing squarely in front of the car, and Cole swears that time slows down, because the man—*No, I don't believe you*—turns, his face registering surprise, and then time jolts again, and the man pivots, running directly into the woods behind the parking lot.

Cole jerks the car door open and runs after him. The sudden softness of grass under his shoes is springy and unsteady, and then the night gives way to whipping branches and leaves in his face. He's pushing through, twisting his ankle in the tangles of downed limbs, trying to see in the dark, trying to hear over his own heart and the sound of his body thrashing through the woods, as he yells, "Damon!"

He screams it over and over, stumbling blind in the darkness. He falls to his knees at some point and covers his face with his hands. The night is dark, the woods are thick, and he can't hear anything but his own sobs.

YOU NEVER INTENDED this. He was never supposed to know. Hell, if it comes to intent, then you lack it entirely. None of this is what you imagined when you promised Cole to always be there for him, to never leave him alone. You couldn't have known what you would do to be by his side.

But this—this especially is a mistake. You know it

even as you take the steps through the woods to kneel at Cole's side. You know it as he flinches and then tackles you to the ground, wet tears on his cheeks brushing your own as he pins you. He puts his hands all over you, feeling your face, your body, and he's saying, "Are you? Are you really? Damon?"

Your heart is pounding, and you can smell him, the scent of shampoo—not the same—and his own particular odor. His body is strong and warm against you. You feel hot and cold, shocked at yourself that you've done this, that you've taken this risk, without a plan, without anything but that restless need that compels you and has from the moment you died. Ever since you found yourself naked and terrified on a mattress in an unfamiliar cabin, you've been driven to stay, to watch, to govern: the need that arches over everything except the need to make Cole's pain stop.

It's so dark in the woods that you can still deny it all, providing you can break free from his grip, but you hear yourself say, "It's me, Cole." He jerks back, letting go of his own accord, putting distance between you. Now is your opportunity. You can go back to hiding, you can run, and this never happened.

But it has, and you can't leave him alone here; he's terrified, doubting his sanity, and you won't do this to him.

"How?" he says, and then he scuffles against the floor of the forest, and you wish you could see him better, to know how he's reacting to you. "No—" he says. "I don't believe you."

"That's what you said the other night," you murmur. "Not a lot's changed."

"You're dead. I *saw you die.*"

You can hear the terror in his voice, the disbelief mingled with hope, and there behind it all, the anger, and the outrage that you could be alive when he's been devastated for so long.

"Cole, calm down," you begin, putting your hands out toward him cautiously, even though you know it's too dark for him to see the gesture. You're shaking yourself, though, and you can't imagine that your touch would be very calming.

"This can't be happening," Cole says, and the tone is familiar, panic-laced, and you remember the end: the pain, the all-encompassing physical pain, the devastation of seeing Cole hurting, the denial in Cole's voice, the fear, and his terror that pierced you even as your body gave out under the stress of the injuries.

Death isn't the land of rest as they claim. Not for you. No, death is so *wrong:* a fever-dream of collapsing atoms, and then an endless, restless knowledge that Cole needs you, that Cole is in pain, that he's suffering, and a driving need to make that stop. There's no peace in death. There's only exhausting, grand yearning, and the never-ending pain of forced becoming.

"It's happening," you say, creeping toward the shadow of Cole panting a few feet away.

"How?" he breathes.

"Not here. Cole, we should leave."

"No," Cole says, backing away from you. "It's a trick. What do you want from me?"

"Cole—"

"Don't say my name like that! You aren't him! He's *dead*. You can go to *hell*. I've figured it out. I know the truth."

You can take this as an out. You know that you can. He's willing to believe this is a delusion or a con, and you can walk away from this blunder, and go back to…to what? What is there for you to go back to? Your life, the very force of it, is focused on one thing: Cole.

You say, "Listen, this is idiotic. The *truth* is that we're in the middle of the woods. It's night. It's cold. And I'm hungry."

"*What?*"

"Let's go," you say, pulling Cole up from the ground. You want to kiss him, to press your body against his and feel him close, to smell, and touch. You've wanted him so much. He's so close, closer that you've dared in all of these months. It feels so right to touch him, even just to hold his arm.

"Who is paying you to do this?" Cole asks.

"How much is *who* paying me for *what*? No one could pay me enough for this."

"Enough for what? I don't understand," Cole says,

and you know that his mind is fumbling for something that makes sense. You understand how he feels, but you don't have time for it right now.

"It isn't a cup of tea," you say. "Come on. We need to get somewhere warm."

"Is this…? Are you planning to kill me?"

"What? Cole—"

You can't talk to Cole here. Not now. You have to get him to leave the darkness of the woods before this conversation can go anywhere. You feel his body trembling under the palms of your hands, but he's not moving away.

"I'm not going to hurt you," you say. You *are* hurting him, though. You've been hurting him since Alex drove off the bridge, and this is a mistake that is hurting him even more.

"Then what—?"

You take a deep breath. "I can explain everything, but you have to come with me now."

Can you explain everything? It's impossible. What's happened defies the rules of reality. You don't believe in it most of the time. It's a dream. Or the neurons of your brain firing as they die, collapsing, and providing you with some kind of extended experience of reality, but it isn't true.

At least that's what you told yourself for months, even as you used the money Alex left behind in a tin box to eat, buy clothes, and to follow Cole around Maryville.

Except for the objective fact that it keeps being true, and you keep on being here, in this body, alive and not at all dead, there is no way that any of this is happening.

"Explain it now."

"No." You draw the word out, let it linger. "Later. This isn't the time and it isn't the place."

He's as frustrating as ever. You just want to get him out of here, someplace where you can see his face, look him over, and make sure he's okay. Someplace where he can see *you* too, where he'll have to admit that this isn't a dream, and that you have a hell of a lot of explaining to do.

You take his arm and pull, dragging him a few steps behind you, and then you feel him balk.

"Come on," you say. "We can't stay out here all night. We need to get warm. We need some light, and I'm sure as hell not waiting for the sun to come up."

Cole's feet don't move, and you turn back around, prepared to shake him, when he whispers, "Damon?"

You step closer. He reaches out to you, his hands run over your face, in your hair, and he makes a soft, shocked noise. "Damon?" he asks again.

"I'll explain everything when we get out of here," you whisper gently, trying to keep him focused, trying to stay focused yourself. It's hard with him so close. You've wanted this so much.

"Is it you?"

You sigh in impatience and frustration, but also

sadness, because this is not ever how you wanted it to be for him, or for yourself, but definitely not for him. You run your hands up his arms; he's shaking all over, and his breath comes in soft, wet hitches.

"Cole, what do you want me to say?"

"That you're him," Cole whispers, but he sounds scared.

Your hands seek his face in the darkness, and you can almost make out the glimmer of his eyes, as your fingers touch his cheeks for the first time in…too long, too damn long, and you stroke your thumb over his chin.

"Oh, God," Cole says, and his voice is broken, devastated. His knees seem to give, because he's in your arms, leaning against you, crying, and babbling incoherently—your name, and curses mostly, but also disbelief, and terrible hope.

"I thought I saw… I know what I saw. You died. Damon, you died."

You help him down to the ground. You're not going anywhere—not right now. He's going into an acute stress reaction, and you're going to have to find a way to snap him out of it, or at the very least keep you both warm until the sun rises. You hold him against your body. This is a bad idea. You know that. You know it even as you turn his head to you and kiss him, letting his words and sobs fill your mouth. His lips are soft and wet, and you love them fiercely. You stroke his face, trying to calm him, kissing him, and murmuring, "Shh, Cole. It's okay. Calm down. It's going to be okay."

He kisses you back, one fist clenched in your hair, and the other grasping your collar, pulling you closer, deeper, and you stroke his cheek, feeling the wet tears on your fingertips. Your gut clenches. His tears always undo you; they always have. Watching him from afar the last many months has been torture for you, seeing how he flounders, how he starts to rise up, and then is felled again.

You only want him to heal, to be okay, and then you can…end this. Whatever this is. It's all you want. It's what made this happen to begin with.

But Cole breaks a little more every day, and you can't keep to just watching anymore. It's why you stepped out, why you knelt beside him, why you're kissing him now.

His mouth rips away from yours. "No!" Cole says, shoving away, panting. "Who *are* you?"

You swallow hard. This is all wrong. You should have waited. Made a plan. If you were going to approach him, then you should have made sure that he could, oh, maybe, *see you*, because he's completely unable to deal with this in the dark.

"Cole—"

"What the hell is going on? Where am I?" he asks, confusion and terror in every word.

Oh, God. It's heart-rending, and you have to make this stop. You don't need him to believe you. Not now.

You just need to get him out of the woods. You touch his cheek, but he knocks your hand away.

You know what you have to do. You stand up. It's hard to walk away from him; you want to slide down next to him on the ground and make soft noises until he calms, but you're the reason he's in this state, and you think that maybe this…this might be the answer.

"Where are you going?" he asks.

"Come with me and see."

"Why should I trust you? You're dead. This is a dream. And I really want to wake up now." He sounds so frightened, so completely out of his head that you fight your instinct to approach again.

"You can come with me now. Or you can stay here and never know. It's your call."

You have to walk carefully, it's dark, and the ground is uneven with downed limbs, and you stumble, but you finally head back the way you both came. Your horrible, half-broken down car is in the two-day pay lot next to the supermarket across from Cole's office, and if he doesn't follow, then you'll use the barely working pay phone to call the police to come get him.

You hear his footsteps, the crunching sounds of acorns and twigs snapping beneath Cole's feet, and you want to stop, to reach behind you and take his hand, but you don't. If he's spooked any more than he is now, he might take off running in the other direction, and that's a risk you don't want to take.

COLE IS WALKING through a nightmare of something worse than fear—it's hope. He really can't handle hope. It's the thing that hurts him more than anything else, and yet he's letting himself get deeper into it with every step forward. He's got his hand thrust into his coat pocket, turning the stone heart there over and over, as he follows this man, this terrible, terrifying man who tastes, moves, talks, and seems to *be* Damon, out of the woods.

As the man in front of him takes those final steps from the bramble and into the parking lot, the world transforms. Cole's headlights illuminate the area around them.

"I left the car running…"

The absurdity of that, mixed with the reality of Damon standing in front of him, blends with the swirling blue and green dots before his eyes, and he's on the pavement.

Damon…*Damon?*…is beside him, making sure his head doesn't hit the ground, and hefting his legs up, bending them at the knee, telling him…what? Telling him to breathe.

"Don't pass out on me now," Damon says.

"Okay," Cole says, but he doesn't even know what that means. "I won't."

"Good," Damon says. "There's no time for that."

"Why?" Cole asks grabbing Damon's arm. "Are you going somewhere? Are you leaving me again?"

Somehow Cole knows that's not coherent, but it's all that matters right now. Damon has come to him, he's crouched beside him, touching his hair, and looking at him with that focused intensity that only Damon ever had, and if he leaves now…if he goes away again. No time for what? Cole runs hot and cold at once. "You can't leave me. I just got you back."

"Shhh," Damon says. "Cole…" He sighs. "Come on, let's get you up."

Cole lets Damon help him stand, and he stares at him. It's a moonless night, but the headlights are more than enough to illuminate Damon's eyes, green and vibrant, so alive, and Cole remembers staring into them as Damon had died, as he'd sobbed uselessly and begged Damon not to leave him.

Cole feels like he's going to fall again, and Damon's grasps his arm, steadying him.

"It's really you?"

Damon nods, swallows, but says nothing.

"Where have you been?" Cole asks, the words finding a way out of his mouth, like thought bubbles in a comic, unplanned and unreal.

"No place I'd recommend visiting," Damon says.

Cole's heart feels stalled in his chest, and the weight is crushing. "Take me with you." Cole leans into

Damon's hand as it comes up to touch his cheek. "Wherever you're going," Cole says. "I don't care. Just take me with you."

CHAPTER 4

COLE IS QUIET as you drive his car out of the parking lot and point it away from town, toward the woods and the cabin that you woke up in six months ago, naked as the day is bright. The only thing Cole says, as you turn up the long, winding, nearly invisible dirt road to the cabin, is, "You were so close? All this time?"

"Some days, I was even closer," you say.

He makes a wounded sound, and you wish that you could take the words back.

It has been six long months of reading Alex's journals, coming to terms with the reality that you exist in a body that you carved for yourself out of someone else's flesh, trying to make scientific sense of the incomprehensible, and keeping your eye on Cole.

Six months of a half-life that you would shuck if you could, like shucking yet another skin, but for Cole, and the connection that has torn your death asunder and brought you back here as a kind of monster. That's what you believe on those days when your scientific mind can accept that any of this is true.

"Tell me about it," Cole says. His trembling hands are around the coffee mug, the steam curling up to his mouth as he sips. "I want to know everything. How did this happen? Where have you been? What does this mean? Why didn't you come to me?"

The questions spill from Cole's lips so fast that you can't answer one before another pops out. He's calmer, though, and while his eyes are over-bright, his cheeks flushed, and, yeah, he's still shaking like a leaf, he doesn't seem on the verge of losing consciousness anymore; it's an improvement. You feel moderately encouraged.

You want to sit next to him on the not-entirely-ratty sofa that you picked up at the North Maryville Goodwill for twenty-six dollars, but you don't want to get used to his scent, his touch, his presence, because this is all still incredibly fresh for him, and there is still a lot of doubt in your mind that he can handle the actuality of your physical form. There are days when you can't handle the truth of your existence, either.

You pull up a chair and sit down across from him, elbows on your knees and your hands pressed together. "One thing at a time. There's a lot of ground to cover here."

"Start at the beginning," Cole says. His voice is trembling, and he's having a hard time with his mug, the coffee sloshing a little over the sides.

You want to reach out and take it from him, but you let the coffee run down the sides and drip on the wood floor.

In the end, it doesn't matter. There are a lot of things that, in the end, don't matter. That's something you always suspected; people invest a lot of emotion in all kinds of idiocy, and you always knew that it was wasted energy, but now? Now there is no question.

Very little actually matters. You know that to be true, because while you've been fighting your way out of the claustrophobic hell of Alex's body, you've been so focused on one pure thing—Cole—that everything else, every other want, desire, resentment, and dream, has dropped away.

You take a breath and say, "I can't vouch for it, but I've been told on numerous occasions by several supposedly well-meaning old bastards that in the beginning there was the Word, and the Word was—"

"Damon," Cole says, his tone irritated and accompanied with his patented eye-darts of annoyance.

You love that look. You've missed it so damn much. Something unclenches inside of you. This is right; this is better. He's calling you by your name, and he's responding appropriately to your jibes.

"I don't remember the car accident," you say. You've gone over this and over this in your mind trying to understand. "I remember Alex driving and his laughter. Then I remember him swerving to avoid a buck. He lost control and I remember knowing it was going to be a bad crash. I remember being afraid." You trail off, trying to remember more details, but it always stops with that gut-wrenching terror, and then nothing.

"You were scared," Cole says, and his voice sounds worn. "I've thought…I mean, I *made* myself think about how you must have felt. How frightened you must have been." He's pale again, and his lips are losing color.

You want to comfort him and pull him close, instead, you say, "Well, that was unnecessarily stupid of you."

Cole *smiles*. Your breath disappears, and your chest hurts. He's beautiful.

"No, it wasn't," he says. "I had to…I had to know. Damon, I've *missed* you."

"I've missed you, too," you say. He can't begin to know how much. Though, when you've told him everything, how it was, feeling the pull of his need across the barriers of Alex's flesh, he might have an inkling, and you won't blame him for hating you. For being terrified of a love so horrific.

"Then where the *hell* have you been?" Cole demands, anger lighting him up. You can see how it strengthens him, and you're glad he's got the energy to ask.

"I've been dead," you say, and watch his face shift through ten thousand emotions.

"Dead?" He sounds confused. It's confusing. You can't blame him for being slow on the uptake.

"You saw me die. You were there. Remembering you, how upset you were as you held my hand and

I…left. It's tortured me." Your throat is tight, and you swallow hard.

"Tortured you?" He's so lost. You start to reach out to him again, but you hold back. He's got to come to terms with this on his own. You messed up badly in the woods, and now you're going to do this right. "No…no…" he says. "You're not dead. You didn't die. You're right here."

"I died. My heart was put in Alex's chest to save his life."

"Yeah," Cole says, breathless, wide-eyed.

"And then I took it back," you say.

COLE IS PRETTY sure this is a dream. Except now that he's seen Damon, he's confused about that. Before, in the darkness, it hadn't been real, hadn't felt like anything but a nightmare, but now here in the light of the cabin, it's starting to seem possible.

"You took it?" Cole repeats, and he's going to stop repeating everything Damon says soon, once he understands. *If* he can understand. Damon himself looks a little iffy about all of this, and it's kind of freaking Cole out. He's on the verge of hysterical laughter, the bubble of it frozen in his chest.

"I don't know how," Damon says. "It's impossible. I can't explain."

"Well, here's an idea: *try*," Cole says, surprised by another flash of anger. He puts the coffee mug down on the floor away from his feet so that he won't accidentally knock it over, stuffs his hand in his coat pocket and grabs hold of the stone heart, squeezing it until the sharp point digs into his hand. He's awake. Right at this moment, he's pretty sure he's awake.

"I can only tell you what I know," Damon says. "It's stingy on the details and it isn't pretty."

"Tell me," Cole says.

"I don't believe in life after death," Damon says. "It's a fairytale concocted to make little kids behave, or to make them feel better about the realities of life. People die. They go away forever. I knew that from the time I was a kid. My grandparents didn't go to some great beyond with halos and barbeques on Sundays. They *died*. And when my favorite aunt died, she didn't hang around and watch over me, either. She was *gone*."

Cole stares at him. Damon's babbling now, talking fast like he does—like he did—when he's nervous and uncertain. Cole wants to kiss him, wants to touch him so badly, just like the very first time he witnessed Damon losing control. But he can't risk it. Cole is sick with fear, terrified of hope, of Damon, who should be dead, of reaching out and there being nothing there.

Damon talks on, "It was what drove me in a way. I knew that every patient I failed to save was wiped out for good. Pfft, gone. No coming back from it. I had a mission to save those kids before that happened."

"Damon," Cole says, and he wishes Damon had shared this with him before. He wishes he'd known this for a long time.

Damon rolls his eyes. It's endearing and it hurts to see. Cole has closed his own eyes and remembered that very expression so many times.

"I don't believe in life after death," Damon says again. "But…I died. It was endless noise and pain. Clawing, scratching, ripping pain." Damon says it like he's listing the symptoms of a patient, matter-of-fact and serious. "There was a glaring light, and a loud, screaming sound of indistinguishable origin, and the sensation of being squeezed. Pressure."

"Squeezed?"

"It was tight, small. There wasn't enough room, and I had to fight for every inch of space."

"Like being born," Cole murmurs, trying to understand, and he feels like his mind is on the verge of getting it.

"I don't do well in small spaces," Damon says.

Cole nods.

"I did anything to get out. I think murderous is a fair term to describe my emotional state and motivation."

"Murderous?" Cole is a parrot. He's a parrot, and this is a dream. He should stop this explanation and kiss Damon now. He should make love to him, like he's done so many times in his sleep, so full of longing and want.

He could wake up at any second. He reaches into his coat pocket again to clench the heart.

"The long and the short of it is," Damon says, "I took Alex's body from him. I stole it. I woke up here on the floor without any recollection of how it happened. I tore his body apart and put myself in his place."

"So much for the Hippocratic Oath," Cole says, though he doesn't know where the joke comes from. He can't breathe, and he feels lightheaded again.

Damon says, "Yeah, well, it's a good thing they can't hold me to it anymore. Considering I'm dead."

"Are you dead?" Cole asks.

It's horrific. He remembers Alex as he last saw him, too thin, and strange. The way his skin didn't seem like his own anymore, and the hunted, pained expression on his face.

"Beats the hell out of me," Damon says, confusion and stress radiating from his wiry body. "Why don't you make that call?" He sighs. "I've come at it with science, I've come at it with logic, and it defies both every time."

"Yes."

The moment hangs, heavy and weighted with all that's been lost, destroyed, and killed. And still, beneath the horror, Cole aches with all they've lost. All they never got to have.

Cole stares at Damon. The solitude of the cabin, the woods around them, stretches out for at least a mile, and he whispers, "I don't know if this is a dream or not, but I don't want to wake up anymore."

Damon's eyes are soft and gentle, full of affection, and Cole never had the opportunity to get used to that before it was taken away, and he leans forward, trying to get closer. "Why aren't you touching me?"

"Do you want me to touch you?" Damon asks. Damon's expression changes, and Cole feels it in his gut—the predatory gaze, the intent. He feels the tug of it in his chest, his balls, and he's still terrified, but he's getting hard, too.

"I need you to," Cole says.

He needs Damon's hands on him, and his warm body next to him. He wants to put his hands in Damon's hair, run his fingers into the kind of shaggy mess of it, and kiss him again. He has to feel him because even with the sight of him right *there*, Cole needs to understand if this is real.

Damon gets down on his knees, creeping toward Cole, too slowly. Cole grabs his collar, the cotton of the button-up shirt crumples in his hands, and he pulls Damon closer, waiting for the moment when he wakes up and he sobs his heart out over the loss. But it doesn't come. Damon's close, closer, and he feels warm and solid under Cole's hands. He's staring at Cole's lips, but he doesn't move, doesn't kiss him, and Cole's waiting for him to do *something*, complete this moment for him, but Damon just tilts his head a little and runs his eyes down Cole's neck and back over his face.

Cole keeps his eyes open as he presses his lips to Damon's mouth, feels the wet, instant response, and he keeps them open as the kiss deepens. He clings so hard to Damon's shoulders that he might be bruising him, but he doesn't care. Damon's tongue is slippery and soft against his own, and Cole crushes Damon to him, kissing him, relieved by his solidity. Damon's eyes fall closed, and he kisses just the way he did before—hungry, eager.

Cole bites down on Damon's lip hard; Damon jerks, and Cole tastes the copper of his blood. Cole pulls back, and Damon's eyes are shocked, underscored by under-standing.

"Yeah, I bleed."

Cole blinks as Damon leans back to press the back of his hand to his bleeding lip. "I'm sorry."

Damon shrugs and starts to stand up. Cole pulls him back down and takes Damon's face in both hands, stares at his eyes, the green just as he remembers, and he gently licks the blood on Damon's lip, tasting it, watching Damon's eyes soften again.

Damon murmurs, "Didn't know you were so kinky."

Cole bursts into tears at that, as startled by his re-sponse as Damon, and he drags Damon closer, burying his face in his neck, sobbing again. He's so scared that he's lost his mind. And he's not sure which is more frightening—the idea that he might be crazy or the idea that this is real. Because Damon has told him…Damon has said that he…that he took Alex's body, took it over, and transformed it, and now he's here and…now what?

"Alex is gone?" Cole asks between crazy, gulping breaths. "You killed him?"

"Killed," Damon says slowly. "Let's see, I took his body, deprived him of his life. Yeah. That word seems apt."

"No," Cole says. "No, you couldn't. He was your cousin. Your best friend. You would have wanted him to live. You wouldn't—"

"You're right," Damon says.

Cole can hear the heart in question beating beneath Damon's shirt. He can put his hand right over Damon's chest and feel it beat.

"I wouldn't. And yet I did." He snorts a laugh. "Manslaughter or body theft? There's no explanation that's pretty or neat. It's gory. Hell, it's wrong. *I'm* wrong."

"No!" Cole says, and he grabs Damon's face. He doesn't understand, and he's not sure he can accept it all, but Damon isn't wrong. He's not wrong. Cole hasn't felt anything so *right* as Damon in his arms, not in two years. Not since he saw Damon's body damaged beyond repair in that bed. "No. Don't say that."

"What do you want me to say? You wanted an explanation. This is the best I can give you."

"I know," Cole breathes, and he feels Damon relax a little against him. "How long?" Cole asks. "How long have you been here, just out of my reach?"

"Six months," Damon says. "Give or take."

"You've been here, living in this cabin, for six months? And you—"

"Well, *I've* been here for six months, but Alex was here longer than that." Damon shifts a little and then moves up to the couch, pulling Cole along with him.

"My knees," Damon says by way of explanation for the move.

For a moment, Cole isn't sure what to do with himself, but then he climbs on top of Damon, who looks a little startled but mostly pleased by Cole's choice. Cole plasters his body to Damon's, feeling the length of him against his own, clinging to his shoulders, pressing his ass back into Damon's groin, and Damon gets hard against him.

"How could you never come to me?"

"What was I supposed to do? Waltz into your house and say, 'Hi, honey, I'm home?' I was *dead*."

"Yes?" Cole asks, breathing so close to Damon's lips, pressing a kiss by the side of his mouth, moving against him, and getting hard again. If this is going to be a sex dream, he really should speed the whole thing up. He doesn't want to wake up before it's too late.

Damon is babbling, though, agitated. "Was I supposed to go to the hospital and tell them, 'Hi, hand over the pediatric charts to the living-dead oncologist. First one to make a zombie joke buys beer!' Go to Emily? Explain to her what I did to Alex? Hurt her like that?

I've seen her, Cole. Who'd believe me? You don't. Hell, even I don't. I don't know what to do."

"Damon," Cole says, trying to calm him, wondering if Damon is always this strange in his dreams. He doesn't think so. Usually they're playing chess, or making love, and this is so incredibly different. This feels so raw and real.

"Cole, I only want one thing. I want you to be happy, and then this can be over."

"What do you mean 'over?'" Cole says. His heart's trip-hammering now, and he's still got his coat on, but it doesn't stop the chill. "I can't be happy without you. I tried. It doesn't work. I need you."

"Ah, Cole," Damon sighs. He brings his hand up to Cole's jaw, thumbs his chin, and says, "You could love him. You could be happy. He seems like a good man."

"What are you *talking about*?" Cole thinks this dream, or hallucination, has taken a very wrong turn.

Things had just started making sense, albeit in a gruesome horror-story kind of way, and now he's lost again. Lost and scared, because Damon is talking about things being over, and what if he wakes up now? He doesn't want to wake up. Not now. Not ever. He wants to take Damon's clothes off, and make love to him, and do all the sweet, dirty things he's always wanted to do, and he wants to walk out of this cabin with him in the light of day, and take him home and keep him there forever.

"The man you were with tonight," Damon says. "You're with him almost every night. You smile. You laugh. I hoped—"

"Michael?" Cole says, and he laughs, but it sounds crazed. "He's my employee. He's a friend, I guess. We work together."

"He's good for you," Damon says. "You look different when you're near him."

Cole says, "He's straight, and I'm not even interested, I mean, I don't want…and he's in love with Emily. You—hoped? You wanted me to—what are you saying? Are you, do you… You don't want me?" He feels the tears coming again, and he can't believe there are any left to cry. But he's wounded now. Damon's returned but not for him, not for him at all.

"I want you so much I killed a man to be near you," Damon says, fiercely. "Stop the waterworks."

"Yeah, well, this is killing *me*," Cole says, brushing the tears away. "I think I've lost my mind."

Damon softens. "You and me both."

"Is it? Is it you and me? Or am I all alone in some mad dream and I'm gonna wake up and this is going to rip me open all over again, 'cause I can't do it, Damon. I can't go through that again."

Cole's still on Damon's lap, still covering as much of him as he can with his body, feeling Damon's face with his fingertips, kissing his lips between words, and rubbing against him. "I can't do this if it's gonna be the same. It hurts too much. I'd rather die."

Damon grips him close, his body starting to respond to Cole's movements, his hips grinding up into Cole's ass. "No," Damon says. "You're gonna have the whole package."

"Damn you," Cole says, breathless. Kissing Damon's neck, tasting his sweat, Cole works to pull off his coat and throws it on the floor behind him.

"Give it to me, then," Cole says, fingers on Damon's buttons, opening his shirt, wanting to feel his skin. "I want everything with you. Only you."

"Cole," Damon gasps, and he's working at the buttons on Cole's shirt, too.

This is more familiar. Cole's used to this in the dreams. It's closer to what he understands, but it's different, too, because in his dreams Damon holds him more gently, not so rough, and he's not as *Damon-like* in the way he kisses, and sometimes, terrifyingly, he morphs into a stranger in the middle of it all, and that usually jolts Cole awake in sick sadness.

But this—this is really real. This feels like nothing he's experienced since Damon's death. It's getting greedy and desperate, and their mouths are fused together, while small noises of need escape them both. Cole gets Damon's shirt unbuttoned first, and he pushes it off Damon's shoulders. His hands go to Damon's chest, mapping the lines of him, and then they brush over the scar.

Cole pulls back, and stares down at the red, thick line down the middle of Damon's chest. He tentatively puts a finger on it and touches the glossy, raised tissue.

"Does it hurt?" He trembles.

Damon takes his hand, runs the tip of his fingers down the scar, and says, "Frankenstein's monster. Proof of my terrible nature."

"Wow," Cole says. "That's where they—"

"Put my heart in Alex's body," Damon says.

"Oh my God." Cole touches the scar again.

He doesn't know why, but it's the scar that makes him believe. It's not a dream. This is reality. And there's no explanation, but Damon is here with him, the real Damon, not a dream or a hallucination, but *Damon*.

He's forced his way through hell, and he's done terrible things, horrific things, to be here with Cole now, and he should be afraid. He should hurt for Alex. For Emily. But all he feels is relief. Huge, sweeping, desperate relief.

"It's you," he says. "It's really you."

"I DON'T KNOW if I should be relieved that you finally believe it's me, or worried that you were apparently under the impression that you might be making out with someone else," you say.

It's a joke. You know exactly how you feel. Relieved.

Deeply relieved, because now he knows, and you have him here with you. Now you can start to do *something* to make him live again. A plan can commence. You're selfish, but you're glad to no longer be alone.

Cole's kissing you again, and he's crying at the same time, which just destroys you. He's got his fingers twisted into your hair, pulling hard, and it hurts, but you don't mind at all, because you'll take whatever he needs to give. This isn't at all how you imagined the night going when you left the cabin earlier in the evening to watch Cole. You only wanted to make sure he was all right, to make sure that he wasn't going to do something crazy like play in traffic again, and somehow now you have him in your arms, and he's letting you push the shirt off of his shoulders, kissing you harder, making your torn lip bleed again. You don't mind.

He's frenzied now, pushing at you until you're lying down on the sofa. You have a bed. It's in the other room. It's got blankets fresh from the laundromat and a space heater to fight the cold night air, but Cole isn't letting your mouth go long enough to tell him.

"I want you," you whisper when he finally moves on to your neck, sucking and kissing hard enough to leave marks.

He whimpers, humping against your leg, burrowing his arms under your body, to hold you tight enough that it's hard to breathe. "Damon," he says, the hot breath against the wet skin of your text. "Need you so much."

You manage to get your hand down to his fly, undoing the button and the zipper, and he lifts up off of you enough to help you push his pants down over his hips. His cock is hot, and your hand wraps around it before he can collapse on top of you again. He shudders as you squeeze.

He always wanted to wait before. He wanted to be sure. You think about asking him if this is what he wants now, but he's moving so fast, rutting into your hand, pawing at your body, rough and needy. You run your hand down his back, and his skin is smooth, soft, and you're surprised by the intense emotion that shocks through you as you touch him.

You can tell he's about to come. He's tensing, holding his breath, and struggling for it, reaching with his whole body, and you're pretty close, too. His hips are angled against your cock, and each downward thrust into your hand pushes against your dick too. He shudders, and his back goes slippery with a fine sheen of sweat now, as you rub your hand up and down, encouraging him to come. This is something you dreamed about before, and you've dreamed about since, and yet this exact situation was not what you imagined. It's more primal. Less romantic. Not how you thought Cole would want to do this at all.

"Damon," he gasps against your neck, shaking and so very close. You have to see his face. You need to know what he looks like when he comes. You shove on his shoulder, pushing him toward the couch, turning so that you're both on your sides, and it's easier to move your hand this way. He's wrecked. His eyes are open, staring at you, and he's a disaster of emotions: love, lust, fear, hope. You don't know that you've ever seen anyone so mixed up, so painfully *needy*, and something in you rises to that, wants to fill that space, make him whole.

He licks his lips, takes your hand in his, and moves it to a different rhythm, faster and rough. You kiss his mouth, and he shudders, twisting his hips, driving his cock recklessly into your loosely clenched fist. Suddenly, he says, "This isn't a dream, right? I don't wanna wake up."

"It's not a dream," you say.

His eyes go to your chest, and his fingers touch the scar, running up and down over it. Then he stares at your face, vulnerable, lost, just as he tenses, gasps, and comes hard, his body jerking and shaking, spurts of come hitting your stomach and sliding down over your hand. You're full of *emotions* seeing this, feeling the heat of his jizz on your skin, the panting of his breath in your face. You love him.

You love him something fierce.

CHAPTER 5

COLE OPENS HIS eyes, and he's still here with Damon. The room hasn't changed or morphed. Damon's still got a blazing red scar on his chest, and he's still there feeling like Damon under Cole's fingers.

Damon milks Cole's cock slowly, pulling the last shudders and drops of come from his body.

Cole pushes his hand away, too sensitive now, and he doesn't mind at all when Damon twines his come-covered fingers into Cole's hair to bring him in for a kiss. He wants to be covered in their sex. He wants to have Damon's jizz and life on him, and, soon, in him. He wants to see Damon's face when he orgasms, and he wants to see it now.

Damon's still moving against him, his own hard cock still trapped in his jeans, and Cole's hand drops down to squeeze it, feeling the outline against the palm of his hand. Damon.

Damon.

He stares at Cole's mouth, panting as he moves, and Cole has to touch him. Has to get his fingers around

Damon's cock, wants to suck him down, get Damon's cock in his mouth, his throat, take him as deep as he can get it.

"Damon," he says. "Let me."

Damon's hands go to his own fly, and he's got his pants down around his hips before Cole can move to help, so he kicks his own jeans down and off instead, lying next to Damon again, naked and still mostly hard.

Damon drags his fingers though Cole's chest hair, pulling gently, and Cole shivers, looking down between them to Damon's cock jutting up against his stomach. This is no dream. Damon's cock is nothing like he imagined. It's thick, and the curls at the base are a dark auburn, and in his dreams Damon's cock was always just *in him*, sometimes gentle and sometimes rough, but never quivering in his hand and leaking a pearl of pre-come from the engorged tip.

"Cole," Damon grits out. "Are you just gonna look at it?"

Cole laughs, a soft sound that rips out of him in amazement, and he feels so high, like he's falling through air and there's no bottom to hit. It's crazy because this is the first time he's felt this way in *years*, like he felt when Damon told him that he loved him, like he felt when Damon told him that he was willing to wait as long as it took for Cole to be ready. He can't start to cry again, not now, but this is *joy*, and it's fucked up because this is *insane*, but he's got Damon's cock in his hand and his other arm is twisted up to pull at Damon's hair, and he loves him so *much*, and he's wanted this so *long*.

"God, Damon."

"It's big, I know," Damon says. "Stunning, I'm sure. But do something with it before I do it myself."

Cole laughs again. "Damon…Damon." He keeps saying his name, because he *can*.

He leans forward and kisses Damon's mouth, twisting his wrist and pumping his hand over Damon's cock. Things get so hot so fast, with Damon thrusting into his hand, and tugging at Cole's body, bringing him up tight so that Cole barely has room to move his hand. Damon's got his mouth open on Cole's neck, sucking hard and strong, sucking and biting, and Cole's shaking, holding Damon's mouth against his skin, squirming against the pleasure-pain. Cole feels Damon's cock swell and pulse against his palm. He holds Damon as he jerks and quivers, his come smearing between their stomachs heaving against each other.

"I love you," Cole whispers. "I love you, Damon."

"I love you, too," Damon says, his breath puffing against the sore place he made on Cole's neck. Cole closes his eyes. Nothing matters but right now. He can die happy. He's here with Damon and this, *this moment*, is all that matters.

COLE'S WET FROM the shower, and Damon's got him in his bed now, wrapped up in blankets. The space heater is turned up high, battling the cold that is seeping under the doors and through the windows. Cole's also hungry, which Damon has declared a good sign, and so Damon's in the kitchen making sandwiches for them both. From his spot on the bed, Cole watches as he drops a piece of cheese on the floor, and bends to pick it up, his ass outlined in the loose sweats he's wearing, and when Damon turns to throw it in the trash, Cole can see his nipples are hard and he's shivering from the cold.

It's painful to have Damon in the other room, but Damon's declared that Cole must stay warm, and that where he wants him most is in his bed. Cole feels the distance like an ocean between them, and so he pulls the blankets around himself to join Damon in the kitchen. That's when Damon turns around, slashes his butter knife through the air, and says, "Don't even think about it."

"Damon," he whines, wheedling, thinking the sandwich is pretty unimportant now. He just wants Damon next to him. He wants to run his hands over him, make sure that he's real again.

"Almost done," Damon says, squirting mustard onto a piece of bread, and slapping mayonnaise on the stack of meat, and tossing all the fixings back in the old, banged-up fridge. He grabs two bottles of water and tucks one under each arm, turning around with two plates full of giant sandwich.

As Damon walks toward him, Cole reaches up to touch the love mark on his neck, feeling the bruise, remembering the red glare of it in the mirror, stark against his white skin.

"You liked it," Damon says, nodding toward where Cole's fingers are mapping the wound.

"It feels real," Cole says.

"Looks real, too," Damon says, putting the sandwiches down on the bed, tossing the water against the pillow, and leaning over to check Cole's neck. "I didn't break the skin," he says. "That's good. Here, let me see your head."

"It's nothing," Cole says, batting his hand away from the bruise on his forehead. "Just a concussion." Saying the words aloud unnerves him. He's got a head injury. Can he trust himself? Is he sure that this is real?

"'Just a concussion,'" Damon mocks. "Head injuries are never 'just' anything. No double vision? Headache?"

"I'm fine," Cole says, but his voice sounds uncertain even to himself, and Damon's eyes narrow. "Hallucinations are associated with head injuries," Cole says slowly.

Damon nods. "Lucky for you, this isn't a hallucination. Though maybe it would be better for both of us if it was."

"Don't," Cole says, denying it.

Damon leans close, and Cole can smell his skin, warm and fresh from the shower. Damon's lip is swollen from his earlier bite test, but it's stopped bleeding. He takes Damon's chin in his hand and looks at the small wound. "What about your lip?"

"Mouths heal quickly," Damon says, dismissing Cole's worry. "Here. Eat this."

Cole accepts the plate that Damon thrusts at him and holds it on his lap as Damon climbs beneath the covers beside him. Damon's muscles move under his skin as Cole watches him get settled. His skin is soft, freckled lightly on the shoulders, and Cole wonders if he freckles more in the summer. He almost starts to cry again because now—*now he can know.*

Damon takes a huge bite of the sandwich, chews it, swallows, and takes another. He motions at Cole's plate and says with his mouth full, "Eat."

Cole doesn't know if he can manage it. He was hungry before, but now his appetite is gone again, even looking at the sandwich makes his stomach balk. He feels wired, like every inch of him is on watch, and that if he relaxes even a little then all of this might disappear in a wave of despair.

Damon swallows. "It's a perfectly good sandwich and you're wasting it."

Cole shifts closer to Damon so that his hip presses against Damon's, the soft sweatpants warm against his leg, and he manages about four bites before he's unable to force another.

Damon looks at the sandwich and then at Cole.

"You need to eat, even if you don't feel like it."

"Is that a medical opinion, Dr. Black?" Cole tests it out. Is this okay? Can he do this? He lets the name roll off his tongue. He hasn't said it in a long time. It feels good.

"No, *sweetheart*," Damon returns. "It's this little thing most idiots call common sense. Though, given your behavior on the road the other night, I'm thinking that particular evolutionary advantage skipped you entirely."

"It was stupid," Cole says.

"Damn straight," Damon agrees.

Though if he hadn't been walking on the side of the road, tempting fate to do him in, then he wouldn't be here with Damon now. He knows this. And he won't regret it.

"I'm not sorry."

"I didn't ask you to be," Damon says, taking another bite of his sandwich. He chews, sighs and swallows as he looks up to the ceiling. "Ah, all of this *drama* has worn me out. I say we eat and then go to sleep. There'll be time for more of this tomorrow."

Cole doesn't want to sleep. He doesn't *ever* want to sleep. In fact, the thought threads his veins with ice-cold terror. He can't risk that he'll wake up in his bed, or in the hospital, and find that all of this is a fever dream or the result of the head trauma. He knows it's irrational, but his current plan is to stay awake for the rest of his life; he's not sleeping ever again.

Damon has finished his sandwich, and Cole can't believe it, but he says, "Well, if you're not going to eat it—" and he takes the sandwich from Cole's plate, taking a massive bite out of the side.

"You're ridiculous," Cole says, and he feels like he might start laughing again. The swings in his emotions are wearing him out, it's true, but sleep is not even an option.

"It takes a lot of energy to keep this up," Damon says, motioning to his body.

"You mean—" Cole's stomach tenses, and he feels like he might throw up what little he's managed to consume. "You're still *doing it?*"

"Doing what?" Damon asks.

"You know, still keeping Alex away? Is he…in there?" Cole doesn't know what he'll do if Damon suddenly starts to…turn back. He feels like he might crawl out of his skin just thinking of it.

"I was referring to my impeccable physique," Damon says, but it's clear that he knows it's not at all funny. "No. I don't have to fight for this body anymore," Damon says. "I won."

"So, you're saying, Alex is totally gone? There's nothing left?"

Damon shrugs. He looks stressed, confused, but he just sighs. He puts Cole's sandwich aside, and gets out of the bed, a rush of cold air sweeping over Cole's torso as he does. He runs a hand through his hair before picking up the plates to return them to the kitchen. "No, there's almost nothing. I don't feel him at all."

"Wow," Cole says, and if he's honest, he has to admit that he's scared. It's hard not to think of what Alex must have gone through. He watches Damon put the plates in the small sink under the window. He moves like Damon; there's not a hint of Alex. Cole swallows at Damon walking back with his fluid gait. "So, there's nothing left of him at all."

Damon stands next to the bed. He doesn't climb in. He's studying Cole, and Cole knows that he senses Cole's fear. "There are some journals that he kept," he says. "He may have just been a nurse practitioner, but there was some part of him that understood this transformation was of scientific interest, even if it is impossible." Damon shrugs. "Or maybe he was just trying to understand what was happening to him. Whatever; he kept a record."

Cole can feel how Damon is pulling away from him emotionally. Damon's face goes nearly clinical at Cole's next words. "Show me. I want to see them."

"All right." There's a small table on the other side of the room, stacked with papers and a few composition books. Damon picks the black and white books up, so familiar to Cole from high school and college, and brings them over to the bed. He tosses them down beside Cole and says, "That's all there is. Have at it."

Cole says, "Don't be mad."

Damon uncrosses his arms and drops down on the bed next to Cole. "I'm not. If anything, I guess this emotion is fear."

Cole touches Damon's bare arm, rubbing at the chill bumps, and he says, "What are you afraid of?"

"Are you serious?" Damon asks. He's tense, and he motions at the books. "Those journals…they tell you everything. It's clear what I did to him. I'm a doctor. I've seen a lot of horrific things in my life, and what those journals… Look, it's beyond understanding, Cole."

"You think I'll leave you now? After I just got you back? Over what's in these journals? You don't know me at all, if you think that."

"You haven't read them yet. It's easy enough to say when you don't know." Damon pinches the bridge of his nose and waves toward the composition books. "Just…read them. You should know the truth. This is why I never came to you before. Why I shouldn't have come to you now."

Cole grabs hold of Damon's arm and pulls him into an embrace. He expects Damon to resist, but he doesn't, and the composition books fall to the floor as Cole rolls Damon underneath him, covering him with his body, kissing his neck, his face, the blazing red scar on his chest.

"Shut up," Cole says, pressing his hardening cock against Damon's hip bone. "I need you, and nothing changes it. You could be covered in his blood, and all I'd think is that I'm *so glad*, Damon, so damn glad to see you."

Damon's hard, too, and Cole lifts up to push Damon's sweats down, and then lowers himself so that their cocks rub together with every push and thrust between them. Damon clings to him now really hard, his nails digging into Cole's back and shoulder, and Cole kisses him, licking at the wound on his lip, sucking his lips, wrapping his arms around him and holding him so tight that he knows that it hurts. But he still can't get close enough. He wants to get inside Damon, to have Damon inside of him, but he's too lost in the delicious push and pull of their bodies rubbing together to insist that they do it differently, that they move on to something more advanced than this.

He ruts against Damon, and Damon's stares up at him with wide, green eyes that are full of want and fear. This isn't something Cole ever imagined, but he's honored to be given this part of Damon, this fear and worry amidst the lust, and he whispers, "You can't *make* me leave you. Nothing can. Never again."

Damon nods, and Cole clings to now, concentrating on the pain of Damon's nails on his back, scratching at him with need.

Cole is frantic now, his hips moving fast and hard against Damon's stomach, his cock sliding next to Damon's velvet, hard dick. He grabs Damon's chin, holds his face, and kisses him hard. As he starts to come, he's overwhelmed with an absolute horror that he's made a mistake; he'll wake up this time. He just knows it.

But then gorgeous, jerking pleasure envelopes him, and he's still here, still here, still here in Damon's arms.

Damon's coming beneath him, his face amazingly serious and beautiful as he reaches orgasm. Cole pants and brushes Damon's hair back, touching its springy softness, and kisses Damon's nose, his eyebrows, and his mouth.

As the storm of pleasure calms, Cole collapses, his face buried in Damon's neck. Damon's grip on him gentles. He trembles under Damon's soothing hand, rubbing his back tenderly, and he lies on top of him, not wanting to move. Not now. Not ever.

COLE HAS TO read the journals. It's important to you that he go into this knowing everything. You should have made him read them before you had sex again. Truth be told, you're greedy, and you don't know for sure that he'll want to touch you after he sees the truth of what you've done. No matter what he says now.

You've wanted him for so long, and you never got to have him before. It's addictive. You've come with him twice in less than three hours, and you don't think you're anywhere close to satisfied. You want him again, and thinking about it, you're getting hard again. His body, the way he tastes, the sounds he makes when he's moving against you, and his beautiful face when he comes—you want it so much, you feel starved for it even though you just partook.

"Damon," he breathes against you. "I want you inside me."

You swallow. You want that, too. You want that a whole hell of a lot. And you want him inside of you. Christ, you want to fuck him blind, and then pull out before you come, sink down on his cock, ride him hard until he unloads in your ass, and then you want to plunge back into him and fill him up with your come. You want that so damn much. All your long-held need and desire for Cole consumes you, and the months of isolation and fear while hiding out drives you onward.

"Damon?" he asks.

You take a shuddery breath and say, "I want that, too. But not now."

"No," Cole says. "Don't make me wait. I learned about waiting. It's stupid. Don't, Damon. Please."

"Shh," you soothe, rubbing a hand down his back, feeling his tension. "I don't have condoms."

"Who cares?" Cole says. "I don't care."

"I do," Damon says. "I don't know where this body has been. There were times when Alex was out of his head. I don't know the details of what he did during those times. And—I can't risk you."

Cole makes a sound like he's been kicked, and you

clutch him tight against you, kissing his shoulders, his throat, and the dimple in his chin, loving the scrape of his stubble on your lips.

"You need to read the journals," you go on. "You have the right to know what you're dealing with."

"I'm dealing with you," Cole whispers.

"Yeah," you agree. "And you should know what that is."

"It won't change anything."

"Then reading them won't be a problem," you say. You push at Cole's heaviness, rolling him off, and twisting out from under him. It feels wrong. There's nothing you'd like more than to stay there beneath Cole forever, or at least until you get hungry again, but you're trying to do the right thing.

Cole's flushed up his chest and his cheeks, and his hair is everywhere. There's drying come smeared on both of your stomachs. You crawl out of the bed, saying, "Stay here. I'll get something to clean up."

"Hurry," Cole says, and you know it's not because he's so eager to wipe the evidence of your sex off of his skin but because he doesn't like it when you leave his sight. You can see how nervous he is that this will somehow turn out not to be real.

You wet a washcloth in the small bathroom sink. The cabin isn't luxurious, and you have no idea how Alex even knew of its existence, but it has served you well the last few months. It's small, but not too small, and set far off the road. There isn't much as far as heating goes. You had to pick up some space heaters from the Goodwill in North Maryville, but it's on well-water and a septic system that seems in good working order from what you can tell. Alex certainly knew what he was doing when he came here.

You splash some water on your stomach and cock, trying to get the come off. You jerk at the chill and swallow back a yelp. It's not as warm as you'd like, but the hot water tank usually takes a few hours to replenish itself after a shower, and you and Cole took your time in there together. You'd been tempted to suck him off, but you'd settled for washing his hair and letting him touch you all over.

"Damon?" Cole calls, and he sounds a little worried. That feeling inside of you, the one that used to be so strong that you couldn't stand it, so strong that you fought tooth and nail and emerged with bloody claws, even if you have no memory of the process—that feeling rises up again, and you have to go to him, to soothe that pain in him.

"I'm here," you say, emerging with the wet cloth.

"It's cold," he hisses as you swab the sticky come from the hair on his belly and chest. It's already drying on and it's hard to get off. It would be easier if the water were warm.

"Colder than a dream would be," you say.

"Yeah," Cole agrees. "I think I'm past thinking it's a

dream now."

You touch his face and kiss his lips tenderly. "Good." Though you wonder if he'll regret that in a few minutes.

You bend to the floor and pick up the composition book labeled with a giant black number 1 made in Alex's hand with a sharpie pen. You climb into the bed next to Cole, pulling the covers up around you both, and hand the book over to him. "Fun bedtime stories," you say. "Enjoy."

Cole holds the journal in his hand like he's not sure he wants to touch it. Finally, he opens the first page, and he begins to read.

You watch his face, and when his eyes go wide and his lip goes between his teeth, you know that he's reached the part where Alex describes the pain the transformation caused him, the internal stabbing sensations, the blood running from his nose, eyes, and ears, and the agony of it all.

Time is lost for me. I scream in pain. I want to die but can't find a way to make myself end my torture. Every time I attempt suicide, I am stopped by this demon heart. I wake up hours later still screaming, whatever instrument I've chosen for my death is destroyed and useless, or simply gone. He won't let me go.

You now have reason to hate your excellent memory.

"Oh my God," Cole murmurs as he reads on.

You sit back and wait for him to finish. It's a strange read, you know, with Alex's handwriting twisting in and out from his own to something similar to Damon's and back again.

Alex describes it in detail—not only the physical pain, but the agony of leaving Emily, and his family, knowing that they must be scared and hurting because he's vanished, but also knowing that he can't go back to them, that what is happening is so far out of his control, so far outside of reality, that it will only make them hurt worse to see his agony and his pain. *He won't stop until he owns me.* You remember how true that was, though you had no idea what that actually entailed as you fought so hard to destroy him.

You close your eyes and remember the words that Alex wrote, knowing by Cole's noises, and the subtle way he shifts away from you, that he understands now. He's filled with the terror and horror of what you are, what you've done, and you don't blame him at all. The days that you've spent trying to understand, doing tests, cutting small wounds into your inner thighs to see if they bleed, to see how they heal, and any number of scientific attempts to prove that this is not happening, all lead back to the knowledge that you exist against nature. You should not be here. This was Alex's life to lead. You wanted that for him. And yet you viciously rose up and stole it from him. For what?

You open your eyes and look at Cole. His eyes are glossy, and his mouth is open with shock. He's absorbed in the journal, and he's shaking again.

For Cole.

This is for Cole. You hate that he knows it as well. You wish you could have spared him, but the reality is something he must deal with, just as you do. He's owed that, and you need him to know.

He looks up at you with bright eyes. "Damon…" He sounds like he's going to pass out. "Damon, this is all my fault."

You should have seen this coming.

"Don't be like that," you say.

"It's true. I wanted you so much. I made you have to come to me."

You roll your eyes. "Did you also force me to have feelings for you? Did you make me love you so much that I killed a man to get back to you? Come on, Cole. Your control issues really don't belong in this discussion. So, bzzzz, wrong answer. Try again."

"Would you have…come back or…killed Alex if I was…happy? If I'd been in love with Michael? Like you say you wanted? Would this have ever happened?"

You rub your forehead. He's so infuriating. Sometimes you have no idea what you love so entirely about him. He's bad at chess, and melodramatic, and thinks he controls the universe, or can influence the laws of nature with the force of his love. Never mind that he apparently *did* actually manage the latter, at least in conjunction with your own intense attachment to him, but you can't let him focus on these things. He'll make himself crazy with guilt.

"I never said I *wanted* you to be in love with Michael," you say, concentrating on the one aspect of that comment that you can readily clarify. "I said I *hoped* you could love him."

"*What?*" Cole's shaking his head and getting worked up.

You want to say something to calm him down, but you're going to offer him truth instead.

"Cole, listen, this—me and you, right now? This isn't what I wanted for you. I can't go back to Maryville or even to the world. You *know* that. I love you—and you deserve a life like you've always wanted—"

"I want a life with *you*."

"I know," you say. "And…I know now that I was wrong. Being with Michael isn't an option for you or for me. Dealing with the truth of me, it's not what I wanted for you, but that doesn't matter now, does it?"

"Well," Cole says, swallowing. "No. It doesn't. What matters is what I want, and what you want—and you can't tell me that you don't want me." He waves the journal in the air. "You…you did this to Alex because you wanted me. And…God, Damon." He's on the verge of tears again, and you touch his cheek because his tears always rip you up. "All I want is you."

You rub your fingers against his stubble. You let out a slow breath. "There are three more," you say.

His chin is trembling, but he nods with determination. "Give me the next one."

You hand it over and wait. It only gets worse, you know, but as Cole reads, you see him toughen up before your eyes. His face grows stony, his jaw sets, and when he finishes the second journal, he takes the third from you without a word, radiating a horrible strength.

COLE KNOWS THAT he should be tired, but he's not. He feels like he's had twenty cups of coffee, and he's horny as hell. It's shocking to him that he's reading all of the terrible stuff that Alex has written, and he still wants to push Damon down on the bed and suck his cock, climb on top of him, and ride him hard. He's honest when he says that even if Damon were covered in Alex's blood, he wouldn't feel any different.

The fourth journal is very short. Only about twelve pages, and then there are five pages with two words written over and over.

Help Me
Help Me Help Me Help Me Help Me

There's no punctuation; each plea is scrawled any which way across the page, sometimes overlapping with others. Cole knows that it wasn't written as a chant but as an intermittent plea in the midst of a sea of great pain and horror.

He closes the journal, puts it on top of the small stack, and lets out a long breath. "So," he says. "He's gone?"

"Completely," Damon says. "Apparently, like with everything I do, I was very thorough."

"The amazing Dr. Damon Black," Cole says with shuddering awe bordering on terror. "Accomplished at everything he sets his mind to…or, in this case, his heart."

Damon's expression isn't proud at all. He looks conflicted, tense, and Cole puts a hand on his arm, strokes up and down. His skin is soft, and the hairs of his forearm tickle Cole's fingertips. The humanity of his lover tames his own fear.

Cole asks, "Do you know how this works?"

"How this works? I've already told you I don't."

"No, I mean—do you age? Or, are you…always going to be like this?"

"I've somehow taken over his body, not become an immortal," Damon says in irritation.

"Oh, *sorry*, Dr. Black. I'm just trying to understand." Cole's tone echoes Damon's.

"Well, suffice it to say that I'm not a zombie, I don't suck blood—that's apparently *your* kink—and there won't be anyone trying to cut off my head, declaring 'There can be only one!'" Damon sighs. "I'm worse than any of that."

"And you say *I'm* dramatic," Cole says. "Get over

yourself. You're not that big of a bad." But he is that big of a bad and Cole's insides shake with guilt and the natural fear of prey before a tamed predator.

Damon narrows his eyes and asks suspiciously, "Did you watch Buffy?"

Cole is so surprised and nervous that he starts to laugh. "The Vampire Slayer? No. Did you?"

Damon waves a hand at him and says, "Vices. Everyone has them. What's important here, Cole, is that you accept the seriousness of this situation. I'm not safe here. I'm not safe anywhere. This doesn't end up with a happily ever after."

"I know that, Damon." Cole sighs. He's jittery and he's wild still, but he knows that in the last six hours his life has changed utterly, and he's so damn glad for that, no matter the cost. "I'm not stupid."

"Of course not. I wouldn't even like you if you were."

"Much less have taken a man's life to kiss me again."

"Well, you've got an amazing kiss," Damon says, looking Cole up and down. "And you're kinda hot."

Cole knows he should be horrified that they're smiling about this, smiling about something that took a man's life, and yet he can't help the joy flowing through him. It's Damon. It's *Damon*. He's still so entirely *Damon*.

Cole knows that if it were different, if Damon had actively chosen this, then it would be different. Then Damon wouldn't be the man he loves, he would be a true monster. But this…this was without intent. An accident in a way. No more Damon's fault than the car accident that took Damon's life. Only this time, Damon was the car barreling through Alex, all force and no purpose. Brutal. Violent. Senseless. And blameless.

As Cole's stomach curls with renewed lust, and Damon leans toward him, Cole's cell phone rings. It's the middle of the night, Damon said earlier, but Cole has no idea what the time might actually be. He knows, though, that it's someone in his family, calling to check on him, to find out where he is.

"I should get—" Cole begins, and then he stops.

If he answers the phone, then he has to tell them something. If he doesn't, they'll worry. He's been acting far too strange, more than usual, and they'll probably send the police looking for him. Sheriff Hunt will remember what he was in the station for, Rosanna will get involved, and hell, they'll probably end up calling his dad too, and all of this before morning.

"What am I going to tell them?" Cole asks.

Damon says, "You could tell them the truth—if you want to be institutionalized."

"Yeah, thanks," Cole says, climbing out of bed. He reaches his coat, still on the floor where he dropped it earlier. He fiddles in his pocket for the phone, sees the caller ID, and answers with the most insincerely nonchalant, "Hey, Rosanna," that he's ever managed.

"Cole, honey? Where are you? Dad says you aren't

out at the cabin. Michael said you were acting very strange today at the office…and, baby, it's nearly three in the morning and you aren't home yet."

Cole wants to ask how she knows, but he suspects she went over there when he didn't reply to her earlier texts.

"I'm sorry, Rosanna," Cole says, scratching at his head. He glances at Damon who's staring at him intently. "I should have called. I met up with an old friend. I'm at his place."

"An old friend? Who?" Rosanna asks.

He's not sixteen anymore. He has a right to be anywhere he wants to be. And yet he finds himself making up a lie instead of just telling her that it's none of her business. He doesn't want her to be frightened, and she sounds really worried. "Just an old friend from college. You didn't know him."

"Cole, I'm—"

"Rosanna, I'll see you tomorrow," Cole says, and it feels like another lie, because he's not sure he's ever leaving this cabin again. He's not sure he wants to.

"Honey," Rosanna beings.

Cole cuts her off again. "Rosanna, I'm okay. All right? I'm gonna stay here tonight." He fakes a yawn. "In fact, we're gonna hit the sack now. See you tomorrow."

He hangs up on her before she can say anything else, and he sets his ringer to silent mode so that they won't be interrupted again. He feels like someone reached into the bubble he's been living in the last few hours and popped it. Reality is lies. Reality is his sister being scared for him, and his family being worried. Reality is that he has no damn clue what they are going to do now.

Damon's watching him from the bed, his chest and arms resting outside of the covers. The red scar running down the middle looks dark in the low light. Cole sighs, runs a hand in his hair, and says, "Damon, what are we going to do?"

"It doesn't matter now," Damon says. "You need some rest. You've got to be exhausted."

Cole is—he's so tired. Somehow he's crashed. He was incredibly high before. Higher than the last layer of the stratosphere, nearly floating into space, and now he is here on earth with a not-dead lover, and he's living in a horror story that should scare him to death but only makes him sure that change has come. He's going to have to jump into the fray and beat back the real world with a sword until he can make this right. For both of them.

CHAPTER 6

YOU FALL ASLEEP before he does. You try not to, but you do. You're both sticky with come—once again, you never made it past rutting together, both of you too desperate to even manage a blow job—and you've given up on trying to get it off. You'll deal with it tomorrow in the shower, but for now you give in and let the darkness carry you into dreams.

Sleep isn't comfortable for you; it's too full of what you went through to get here, and you often wake up wet with sweat, as though you're still fighting for your life, battling your way out of Alex. It's necessary, though. You tried to fight sleep in the beginning as a test to see if you were real, because surely, in a dream, you'd have no need for rest, but it always overtook you in the end.

You wake up after only a few hours, and the morning light is coming through the window. Cole's not asleep. He's sitting up in the bed, staring at you and the expression on his face is determined, possessive, even.

You say, "Go to sleep."

He shakes his head, not saying a word. There's no

arguing with him, you know that, remember it well, and you're awake now anyway.

You drag yourself up to a sitting position, rub at your eyes, and say, "You okay?" He swallows and nods, remaining silent, but his expression is intense.

"Cole?" you ask.

He doesn't speak.

"Cole? Hello?"

"Yeah," he says. "I'm just thinking. You're…not…right. Not safe. You're not supposed to be here. It's true. And I know now what I have to do."

You aren't expecting this, but it's not like it's a lie. "Okay," and you drag it out a little. "And what's that?"

"I have to go home." He's nodding, staring at you like he can see your brain through the backs of your eyes. "Then I have to go to the office. I have a lot of work to do there."

When you went to sleep, he'd seemed okay. Wired, yes, worried, yes, and incredibly affectionate, yes, but, in general, Cole had been okay when you fell asleep. Clearly, something has changed in the meantime.

"Yeah," Cole goes on. "And I have a lot of phone calls to make."

You're sure that he probably does. He's a busy guy. But, really, this is so far from what you expected from him this morning. Though when you think about it, you're not sure what you'd anticipated. Wake-up sex? Probably. That was definitely on your imaginary agenda.

"And then I have to go to see my father."

"Cole," you say. "I understand that you're confused. But if you tell Dad about this—"

"No," Cole says. "I won't tell Dad." Cole sounds like he's ten thousand miles away, and yet he's looking at you like you're the only thing he can see. "I can't tell anyone, can I?"

"No."

"Because even if you're right next to me…" Cole swallows hard. "Even if they see you with their own eyes…"

You shake your head.

"Right. It's too much."

"They'll try to explain it."

"Or test it. Test *you*." Cole touches your cheek. "They'd take you apart to try to figure you out."

"Yes," you say.

"I won't allow that."

"You couldn't stop them."

"No, but…" Cole sighs. "No."

"But you don't have to live this way with me. You can return to your family and your life. Walk away from me. I'll understand."

"I can't walk away from you. Not while you're living."

"But if I'm dead?" You are technically dead, and, you assume, there are ways for you to be deader.

Cole's lost in his own head, though, and he just nods.

You're getting nervous now. If Cole decides to end you, as unlikely as that seems, if that will bring closure to him and to you, then you can accept that. Logically. Emotionally, not so much. You're definitely feeling the urge to flee, or to fight, or to at least shake Cole and say, "Do you know what I did for you?" But you stay silent, waiting for more information.

"I hate asking him to do this for me, but this has to be done."

"Okay, okay," you say, holding up your hands. "Back up. What in the hell are you talking about?"

"I'm talking about the plan, Damon. Try paying attention for a change." You blink, and Cole smiles. "You should see your face," he says. "You're scared, but it's all right. I have you now. You should have more faith in me. So many doubts are swimming in your eyes."

Relief floods you like cool water, and you sigh, lifting your hands and letting them fall. "I can't imagine why. You're the most frustrating person I've ever met."

"Have you not met yourself?" Cole grins. He shoves you down against the mattress and climbs on top again.

"So, there's a plan?" you say.

"Yeah," Cole says, mouthing at your ear. You shiver. "I think I left out an important step, though."

"Mmph?" you ask as Cole kisses you.

"Yeah, I need to buy some condoms."

You're not sure what you think of the rest of Cole's plan. It sounds risky from what little Cole tells you when the sweat is once more cooling on your bare skin. You want to work through the details together. You don't intend to be left out of this, not if you can help it, but you can get on board right away with the condom plan. That's a definite yes in your book.

COLE HAS A really hard time leaving the cabin. He's past thinking this is a dream, but he doesn't know if that belief will hold once he can't reach out and touch Damon any longer. He also doesn't trust himself right now. He's sure to give something away with his body language, and the last thing he wants is to make anyone more suspicious than they already are, or will be, if everything goes as planned.

Damon is skeptical, and Cole understands. The day before, neither of them could have imagined that today would be completely different from all the ones since Alex drove off the bridge. It's a lesson that Cole learned when Damon died, and it's so much easier to accept that everything has turned at a moment's notice, because this time, *this time*, Damon is alive. He's *alive*.

And Alex is dead.

Damon walks him out to his car, and Cole stands there, unable to get in. He reaches instinctively into his coat pocket to touch the stone heart, and his other hand raises to his neck, feeling the mark that Damon left there, just barely hidden under his collar. He can still taste Damon's come in his mouth from the blow job in the shower, and he can close his eyes and feel Damon's hands in his hair as he'd curled over Cole's bobbing head and come down his throat. God, it had been so good. Shockingly so after all the worried imaginings he'd put himself through during the year of their relationship and then after Damon's loss.

He should stay. Go back inside and suck Damon off again. He's a jumble of nerves. What if he leaves, and when he comes back Damon is gone? What if the cabin doesn't even exist?

"I'll be here," Damon says, as though he can read Cole's mind. "Even if you return with a mob of villagers carrying pitchforks and torches to destroy the monster, I'll be right here. Not going anywhere."

Cole nods.

"And," Damon says. "My car's in the Save-A-Lot parking lot. Kind of a far way to go on foot."

"Jerk," Cole says, feebly punching him in the arm. His heart's racing a mile a minute, and he doesn't know if he can actually do this. It's too soon. He needs another ten years with Damon before he's going to be ready to drive away from him like this.

"It's only a few hours," Damon says.

"Being so blasé doesn't make me feel any better about leaving you here, you know."

"Should I wail and cry and beg you not to go?"

Cole snorts a laugh and shakes his head slowly. "No… just, you know, act like you—"

Damon grabs his face and kisses him so hard and desperately that Cole's knees give out, and he's left clutching Damon's arm and the open car door for support.

"There," Damon says, caressing his cheek. Cole can't stop the wounded sound that escapes him. Oh God, he can't leave him. Not for a few hours. Not for ten minutes. What if he's gone again?

"Cole," Damon says. "I'm not going anywhere."

Cole nods. "And those condoms won't buy themselves."

Damon smiles. It's brief and sharp, and Cole's stomach clenches with the love of it.

"There'd be a lot fewer teen pregnancies if they did," Damon says.

"I love you," Cole says.

Damon's eyes soften and he touches Cole's chin, running his thumb over it, and he says, "You're my heart."

Cole grins, and he takes Damon's hand and kisses it. "Yeah, I know. Promise me you'll be here?"

Damon glances around. "As long as Alex doesn't come looking for me to claim his body back, we should be good to go."

"Not funny, Damon."

"I'm a barrel of laughs and you know it."

With every exchange, Cole feels less and less able to leave. He's got to rip the Band-Aid off and do this thing. If only to get condoms, he tells himself. He could just get them and come straight back. He touches the stone in his pocket again. He pulls it out and holds it out flat in his hand.

"Evidence of an irrational bout of rampant sentimentality," Damon says, gazing at it, his hands shoved into his pockets, and a speculative expression on his face.

Cole closes the heart in his fist and says, "You left it for me on my doorstep?"

Damon looks down and then up at Cole. Damon seems unsure in that way that makes Cole want to protect him, the way that no one else ever got to see, and so few people would even believe were true of Dr. Damon Black. He says, "You were hurting. I didn't know what else to do."

"It's kept me sane," Cole says.

"Is that what they're calling it these days?"

Cole laughs softly, puts the stone back in his pocket, and says, "Thank you."

Damon says, "It was a mistake."

"Yeah?"

"Best mistake I've made."

Cole forces himself to climb into the car, stick the keys in the ignition, and suddenly Damon pulls the door open. He kisses Cole again and then again. Damon looks at him long and hard, says, "I love you, too," and slams the door.

Damon turns his back on the car and walks toward the cabin. Cole waits until Damon shuts the cabin's door before he starts the car and turns around in the dirt to head down the driveway toward town.

COLE'S STILL ANXIOUS as he walks into the drug store to buy the condoms. He's getting them first because there's no telling when he might freak out and have to head back to the cabin just to make sure that Damon's really there and still completely alive.

He can't decide where he should go first after the store—to Rosanna's apartment or to his father's cabin. He's going to have to tell them both in person that he's leaving. And he'll have to talk to Michael and Emily, too. He'll have to be good to get the truth past Michael. He sees a lot, and he's tough to fool.

Really, though, this is all just the footwork. He can't imagine that he'll be able to follow through on his plan for at least a month, three weeks at the soonest. God, how is he going to manage that? He can't be apart from Damon at night for the next three weeks. He'll have to come up with something. Some reason to not be at home. Especially when they'll all want him around for a while. To coddle him before saying goodbye.

He decides to start with Rosanna. She's the one most

likely to freak out, and if he still has his dad to tell, then he can use that as an excuse to get out of there if she starts to drag it out too long, and he needs to get back to Damon.

Cole is shaking as he pays for the condoms and lube. He can taste Damon in his mouth, and his fingers itch to press on the bruise on his neck again, but he settles for putting his hand in his pocket to hold the stone heart. After this, he needs to walk over to the pay-lot and put another three dollars into the slot for Damon's car. It's the brown Honda, Damon had said. Cole feels crazy thinking that Damon's been driving around Maryville in that car, that he could have passed Cole on the street so many times, and Cole never knew.

He throws a pack of gum on the counter, too, and hands the clerk another two dollars. He doesn't want to erase the taste of Damon's come from his mouth. It makes him ache inside to think about it, but he's about to go see his sister, and he doesn't feel right talking to her while tasting Damon. He pops a piece of the gum, wincing as the remnants of Damon vanish in a wash of mint.

Cole jumps when someone tugs on the back of his sweater. He almost shouts in surprise, he's so keyed up. Emily and Michael are standing behind him, and they have their arms full of candy and fashion magazines. Cole's pretty sure that most of it is for Emily. Michael doesn't seem like he'd be that interested in fashion, but maybe some of the candy is his. Plus, Michael looks a little beleaguered, so Cole knows before anything is even said that Emily's in one of her moods.

"Hey," Cole says, and he has to admit he sounds jittery. If he can't even greet Emily in the store, he's going to crack entirely when faced with his sister, or, worse, a phone call from his mom.

"What's *wrong* with you?" Emily asks. "You look like you're on drugs."

"What? Of course not." Cole takes the bag from the clerk, grateful that the clerk used the brown paper and not the see-through plastic.

Emily looks from the bag to him, and then her head tilts and a smirk draws up the corner of her mouth. "Wait a minute. Did you *meet someone?* Did you *get laid?*"

"Uh, Emily," Michael says, shaking his head.

Cole rolls his eyes. "Do I ask you about your sex life?"

He immediately wants to bleach his brain, because just thinking that Emily might have a sex life with *Michael,* who's standing there looking worried, leads him to a surprising urge to yell. But he doesn't. He tells himself that Michael is good for Emily, and so if he's touching her, then…oh, God. It could be worse?

"You *did* get laid," Emily says. "Who is it? Come on! Is it that handsome guy? The one at the grocery? The cute checkout boy?"

"Uh, *no,*" Cole says, gripping his bag of condoms. He

glances toward the salesclerk who sold him the condoms and blushes.

"No?"

"No! Besides, I wouldn't…he's not even… I don't have to explain this to you."

Emily makes a face at him and says, "Oh, don't be like that. I'm just glad you're moving on from Damon."

Cole clenches his jaw, glaring at her. His fingers clasp the paper bag so hard that it tears a little.

"Come on, Emily," Michael says. "That's not cool. I'm sorry, boss kid," he says to Cole. "She's…you know."

Cole says, "Yeah, I know."

Emily rolls her eyes. "Cole, I love you, but moving on is a good thing. Even you have to admit that."

Cole presses his lips together to keep from yelling at her. She doesn't know anything at all. She has no idea what Damon has done to be with him again. Who he killed. She's so *clueless*. And, damn, he still loves her so much that he wants her to stay that way.

"No, I don't," Cole says through his teeth.

Emily's eyes flicker a little, and she's worried now, and sorry. He can see that. She's thoughtless sometimes, but he knows that in the end she loves him and hates to see him hurt.

"Cole," she starts, but Michael interrupts.

"Emily, we're going to miss the movie."

"Yeah, okay," she says, and she touches Cole's arm

as Michael pays for the load of crap they dump on the counter.

"You're scaring us, Cole," she says softly. "We just want you to be happy."

Cole lets out a shaky breath and tries out his smile for her. It's a little harsh, but he's got to get this under control. "I know, Emily. I love you, too."

He nods at Michael and heads out the door. When he looks back, she's watching him with sad eyes, and he blows her a kiss. She gives him a closed-lip smile before turning back to Michael and their junk.

The brown Honda is parked in space 71, and Cole shoves three bills into the appropriate slot, allowing them another day before the car will be towed and the owner sought. It's a piece of trash, and Cole can't really imagine Damon driving it. He doesn't actually *want* to imagine Damon driving anything.

The drive to his sister's apartment is terrifying, because it takes him further and further from Damon. He can feel the tenuous link between them stretching, getting thinner the more miles that are put between them, and he fights the urge to go back. He has to get started on the plan. There's no time to lose.

His father's car is in the drive. Cole pulls up next to it and hesitates before getting out. He's disappointed that he's lost a good excuse to leave if things escalate into an emotional mess that he doesn't feel up to dealing with but also sort of relieved that he can do this all at once.

It'll be easier if he doesn't have to repeat himself too much. Two birds. One stone.

"Cole, where have you been? I texted you and texted you." Rosanna crosses her arms over her bosom. "What if there had been an emergency?"

The words nearly freeze Cole in place. Memories tumble over him of texts alerting him to an emergency once, and he's breathless for a second. It's an echo that feels too loud right now when everything has been ripped apart again.

"I'm glad you're both here," he says to them, and he forces a smile, an easy attitude. "I've got news. Important news."

Rosanna looks at their father with that patented expression of concern that Cole's seen on her face so many times when it comes to him, especially after Damon's death. She guides him to sit on her sofa, and his father follow close behind, taking the seat next to him. Rosanna, for her part, opts to stand. Hovering is her specialty.

"Cole, your sister's been worried," his dad begins, and Cole has to fight not to roll his eyes.

Of course, it's how it's always been. Dad deflecting onto Rosanna, and Rosanna not even arguing that Dad's probably been feeding into the whole thing himself. Cole knows. He's seen it enough over the years.

"I know, and I'm sorry about that," he says, smiling and clenching his hands together to keep them from noticeably trembling. "I've been a mess the last week, but that's over."

"Over?" Rosanna asks. "What do you mean? Just last night you stayed over at some…well, who knows whose house, and you didn't even check in! What if he'd been a murderer?"

"Rosanna," Cole says, smiling and forcing a little laugh to make it more authentic. "I'm not sixteen. If I want to spend the night with a guy, I can do that. I'm allowed."

Even if Damon is a murderer in his own way.

Rosanna's mouth falls open. "Dad, aren't you going to say something?"

His dad's looking at him carefully, like he sometimes does, as if he's trying to figure out just who Cole is and what makes him tick. "Rosanna, he's right. He doesn't have to explain himself."

"But Cole," Rosanna says. "It's not like you to behave like that. It's just that—well, sex has always been something special to you, and I hate to see that change."

Cole says, "Rosanna, I'm sorry, but I just don't see how this is your business."

"I gotta say, kiddo. I think Cole's right," Dad says again, putting a hand on her shoulder. It sometimes bothers Cole how he does that, like he's keeping her in line. Though Cole gets it. Sometimes his sister needs to be kept in line.

"But that's not the news," Cole says, smiling and

trying to look as happy as he possibly can. He remembers that Damon is *alive* and that helps. "I've decided what I want to do with my life."

Rosanna looks at their father again, and then back to Cole. "Honey, you're already doing so much with your life. You've got the Appalachian Rainbows and Hardiest Hearts, and you're doing an admirable job with Hart Trucking—"

"No," Cole says. "No, I'm really not. I've been distracted and let the directors handle it. Mom's right."

He hates to throw his mom under the bus, but she's strong. She can take it. And it's necessary. It adds weight and deflects his sister's anger and attention onto their mom, leaving him a lot more breathing room to maneuver. By the time she figures it out, if she ever figures it out, he'll be on his way to a new life, and she'll be powerless to stop it.

"Mom's right about *what?*" Rosanna says, and she's angry now. It's even better than he hoped, and he feels only a little guilty.

"It's time I make a decision about the trucking company. Grandpa didn't give it to me to just barely keep it afloat. I can do better than that."

"Well, honey, Grandpa doesn't—"

Cole interrupts her, saying with excitement, "And Mom's absolutely right, I can't do that from Maryville."

His mother's never said any such thing, but Rosanna will believe that she did. It could take months just to sort this lie out. And there will be so many others to untangle, too, before they get anywhere close to the truth. Which they never will.

"*What?*" Rosanna exclaims, and their dad's watching Cole so closely that Cole knows he has to be good, really good, the best he's ever been.

Rosanna says, "And just *where* does Mom think you have to be to manage a trucking company?"

"It's not about managing it. It's about claiming it as my own. I want to start a fresh branch. Build something new and mine. An offshoot of Hart Trucking. I want to go into shipping."

"*Where?*"

"Somewhere near an international port, for one thing," Cole says. "That's where the best-paying cargo hauls come from, after all. Rosanna, listen, I know you're upset, but you know how hard the last few years have been for me. I need a fresh start. I need to get away from Maryville. From the memories."

"From your *family?*" Rosanna asks desperately.

Cole sighs, and he stands, approaching her with his hands out, begging her with his body to understand. "Rosanna, it's so hard here. I think about Damon all the time. It's not about you, or about the family; I'll always need you in my life. But I have to move on, and I just can't do it here."

Rosanna clutches his hands and tears well up in her eyes. "What about that man you work with? Michael? I thought maybe—"

"No." Cole frowns.

"What about Damon's ashes? You said once that you never wanted to leave—"

"Rosanna," Dad interrupts her. "Cole's right. He's doing something healthy for himself. Don't try to stop him."

Oh, God, Cole's stomach hurts seeing his sister's face, and he feels horrible because he thinks that he's so damn lucky that his father is here after all. He should have known that he could count on his father to support him. He always did.

"Son," Dad says. "Your portion of Damon's ashes will be buried by the waterfall forever. Your life, though—it can't wait." He approaches Cole and puts his hands on Cole's shoulders. "I'm proud of you."

He hugs his dad and holds him tight. He'll miss them. Rosanna gets in on the hug, and Cole kisses her hair, whispering, "I love you, Rosanna."

He'll miss them both so much.

THAT EVENING, AFTER visiting his house and packing up a variety of clothes and pantry items, he drives toward his offices.

"Hey, boss," Michael greets him with a smile. "Working on a Saturday? Got something big on your plate?"

Cole pauses in the doorway to Michael's office. There are stacks of files on his desk, and he grins to see that Michael's already worked through about half a dozen so far, placing them neatly in his out box to be filed.

"You could say that," Cole says, putting his hand in his coat pocket to clutch the rock, the sharp edge digging in. "And you're working on a Saturday? If I didn't know better, I'd think you were flirting with me by showing me your hot work ethic."

Oh, Cole realizes. This must be why people think he's into Michael. Cole wonders how he never noticed that he flirts with Michael? He's not interested, not even close, but something about Michael makes him feel safe.

"Things go okay today? You know, on your date with Emily?"

Michael smiles, and Cole knows that Emily didn't make him wait. "Yeah, of course," he says. "We saw the movie, had dinner, and…" He shrugs. "Well, after that she kicked me out. Apparently, her mother comes over every Saturday evening for dinner?"

"She does," Cole confirms.

Michael grins. "Yeah, so, I thought I'd come in here and work tonight. Try to keep my mind off what I'm missing." He lets loose another sigh. "Emily's amazing."

"Hurt her and I'll have your head chopped off."

"Both of them," Michael surmises, and Cole laughs.

"Yeah," Cole says. "Both of them for sure."

"I promise on my soul to do my best by her, and always send roses whenever I screw up."

"Roses, huh?"

Cole feels himself relaxing again. This is easy, and he's closer to Damon now, can almost feel him over the hills separating them.

"My mother always said that roses make up for most things, and what they don't make up for shouldn't be forgiven anyway."

"That's a wise woman," Cole says.

"What about you? Why are you in so late? I'd think you'd be recouping from whatever happened last night to make you look so wild."

Cole's cheeks heat. And here he'd thought he was pulling this all off so well. "Um…"

"You like this guy or what?"

"Yeah. I think I really do."

"Glad to hear it. If that's the case, then why are you in the office instead of spending more time with him?"

Cole swallows. "Well, actually, there's this thing I have to do. A phone call I have to make. And I should warn you, Michael, if things go the way I anticipate, it's going to change your world, too."

Michael looks wary. He leans back in his seat and frowns at Cole. "Oh?"

Cole nods. "Unfortunately, that's all I can say right now."

"So, this is just a heads up that I should worry start-ing…now?"

Cole says, "No, no. Nothing like that. It's just…" A deep breath settles him. "I'm planning on leaving Maryville. I need to change my focus."

Michael's eyes narrow, and he puts his hands behind his head, rocking in his seat. "Hmmph," he mutters.

"What?" Cole laughs under his breath.

"Just wondering if this has anything to do with the guy from last night and that massive hickey on your neck."

Cole reaches up to touch. His collar's come open, and he can still feel the swollen bite mark. He swallows hard. It's really there. He can feel it, and Michael can see it. He didn't even know he needed the confirmation, but it rushes through him so hard that his knees go weak.

"It might," Cole confesses.

Michael studies him for a long time and says, "Okay, boss kid. Okay."

Cole nods at him and turns toward his own office across the hall.

"Cole!" Michael calls out.

"Yeah?" Cole asks, turning back toward Michael's doorway.

"I just wanted to tell you—anything I can do to help, you can trust me."

Cole lets out a long breath. He believes he can. He rubs his eyes and runs his hand through his hair. "Thank you."

He closes the door to his office and sits down at his desk. He can shift most of this work to Michael. There are only a few things that require his absolute attention, and he finishes them in a hurry, with very little idea of if he even did them right. He hopes so.

He finds the number easily enough. He programmed it into his cell phone ages ago, but he's never once used it. He doesn't hesitate as he presses the call button, though. Twelve and a half years of silence on his part, and he'll break it without a second thought now.

There are two people in his life who can help him. Two people with the power to make this happen. But his mom would never keep her mouth shut, and not because she wouldn't want to help him, but her desire to get back in Rosanna's good graces would end with her spilling everything. There was no telling what the consequences might be. Cole can't risk it.

Grandpa, though. Grandpa owes him. And what he owes can't be paid in the form of a trucking company. Cole's not even sure that *this* will make up for what Grandpa's done, but he has no doubt that Grandpa will jump through these hoops for him. And if that means playing nice with his criminal relative, then so be it. He does what he has to do.

"Hi, yes, this is Cole Hart," Cole says. "I need to speak to the warden immediately concerning my grandfather, Joey Hart."

IT'S AMAZING WHAT some money and an entitled tone of voice can get a person. Cole's surprised that they're willing to allow him access to Grandpa the very next day, and that it only costs him twelve grand to get them to agree to give him and Grandpa one hour of unsupervised time, during which Grandpa will be allowed to place several unmonitored telephone calls on Cole's cell phone.

He's done all that he can do today, and he leaves his office, waving at Michael before walking out.

"Sure, boss! Don't worry about me," Michael yells after him. "I'll just be here slaving away alone, just me and my sexy work ethic!"

Cole snorts and laughs, shaking his head as the glass front doors close behind him, the names of Appalachian Rainbows and Hardiest Hearts emblazoned in the frosted glass.

Cole's twitching now, like he's going through withdrawals. He takes out his cell phone, though, before he pulls out of the parking lot and calls his sister. "Rosanna, hey. I'll be at my friend's house tonight. No—you don't get to know his name. I appreciate that you're worried, but I'm fine. I love you. Bye." She's still talking as he hangs up on her.

"Okay," he says, grounding himself by touching the stone in his coat pocket. He drives toward the cabin, his cock getting harder the closer he gets, and his heart pounding in his chest.

Oh God, what if Damon's not there?

✕

YOU'VE BEEN PACING the house since Cole left. There should be a track worn into the floor from all of your walking. There are times when you feel like he's too far away, and you walk out of the cabin to stand in the drive, trying to get closer to him in town, and then it eases and you go back inside, breathing through the need to be near him.

You don't like this. It's taking him far too long. You roll your eyes at yourself. This is not who you are, not how you operate, and yet now that you've held him in your arms, you really can't cope with him being out of them. You pinch the bridge of your nose and shake your head. This is not what you bargained for when you started dating him after that fateful Halloween party, and that makes you laugh pretty hard because *all of this* is so far outside of what you bargained for when you slapped on that nametag as your costume that it has to be funny or else…yeah.

You open the door and lean against the frame when you hear his car in the drive. Cole's climbs out, slams the door, and runs toward you. You don't move, feeling the space between you closing with each step, and the rightness of it, the jittery feeling under your skin disappearing as he gets near, and the solid, perfection of him kissing you, pushing you backwards into the house, pawing at your shirt, and your pants, trying to get you naked before he's even said hi.

"I take it you missed me," you say when he gives up your mouth to bite along the side of your neck. You work to open the buttons on his shirt. It's a different one from last night. He must have picked up a change of clothes from his house.

"Mmm," Cole says against your throat before pushing your pants down and collapsing to his knees.

"Oh, hell," you mutter as he sucks your cock in deep and fast, and your hands clench in his hair. "Tell me you brought condoms."

He waves toward a brown paper bag that he dropped when he came in, but he doesn't pull off your cock, sucking hard, taking it as deep into his throat as he can manage for a novice. His eyes fall closed, and his lashes lay against his cheeks. His face flushes as he works to unbutton his own pants, shoving them down so that his cock bobs free. You want to do something about it, it's hanging there looking delicious, but then he grabs your ass and pulls you in closer. He sucks faster, and you feel like you might ignite, wanting more of him.

You grunt as your cock hits his soft palette and he chokes, pulling back to dive back down, saliva gushing over your balls as he does. He's so hungry for you, and you throw your head back. It's so good, it's nothing you'll ever be willing to give up now that you've had it, and you're glad that he doesn't know the things you're thinking; the guilt is gone. You don't feel like a monster, and, all of it—the struggle, the horror, the consequences—is worth it for this. For Cole on his knees with this red, slick, hot mouth on your cock, and your legs shaking as the pleasure arcs through your body. *Your* body. It's *yours.* For him.

Cole's worms a finger in between your ass cheeks, and you spread your feet apart more, letting him in. He grunts around your cock as he pushes and you bear down, the tip of his finger entering you, rough and dry. He whimpers as he sucks you, holding his finger just inside your ass; his hips hump the air crazily as he shudders and moans. It's nearly the hottest thing you've ever seen, the way he's giving it up for you, without shame or hesitation, just humping the air like sucking you is going to be enough to get him off.

Seeing that, you're so close. His dry finger twisting in your ass hurts so fucking good, and he's so hot, you would love to come right now, come in his mouth and watch him swallow it down, but more than that, you want to fuck him. You jerk his hair hard and pull him off your cock with a loud pop. He stares up at you, wild-eyed, and shaking.

"Get on the bed," you say, pulling him up with one hand still in his hair and the other tugging at his arm.

You push him toward the bedroom. He kicks off his pants and tosses his shirt on the ground as he goes, and you grab the brown bag from the floor, opening the box as you follow.

You stop in the doorway. Your breath catches, and your cock flexes so hard that you grab it, making sure that you don't lose control now. Cole is ridiculously beautiful. He's so gorgeous that you feel your asshole clench with longing for him to fuck you, and your cock aches to slam balls deep into him, too. You swallow hard, working on control, because Cole's on his back and he's *naked* for you. His cock is rosy, thick, and hard, arching up against his stomach, and he pants, bright-eyed, as he watches you cross to him. You throw the box of condoms on the floor by the bed. You rip open the one in your hand, roll it on your cock, and toss the bottle of lube onto the mattress.

Cole's eyes are hot and desperate, and you don't wait, grabbing his legs and hefting them up, burying your face in his ass, not giving him any time to adjust, just going right to his hole, sucking and biting. He jerks and cries out in surprise. You lick some more, wrapping your arms around his legs, pulling him closer to the edge of the bed so you can get in easier. He's making sounds that you've not heard him make yet, and your cock *aches* to be in there, to be in the sweet, hot place you're eating. He's so tight. So fucking gorgeous. You want him so badly, and this feels right. So right. This is probably the rightest thing you can remember doing since you died, and possibly ever in your entire life before that.

You spit on his asshole and press a finger in. He's tight. Damn tight. And you want to make sure you don't hurt him. It's *Cole*, and you know he's never done this. You're on edge, wanting to shove into him fast and hard, but you work your finger into his hot, tight hole, taking your time. You lick all around, making it wet and slick, and then pull your finger out to kiss and suck some more.

Cole's legs are shaking hard, and he's curling up off the bed as he moans and whimpers, but you shove his legs toward his ears until he falls back against the mattress, and you go back to work.

Eating his ass is the most rewarding thing you've ever done, more rewarding even than getting him off, because you can tell, you *know*, that he never knew this sensation before. He's sobbing and twisting, and it takes all of your strength to hold him down as you press your tongue in, feeling his hole twitch against your mouth. He's *wild*, begging you, tugging at your hair, and you let him pull all he wants. You lick and suck, getting him slippery and wet. It tastes intimate and intense, and you want to share it with him, to push up and kiss his mouth, but you can't make yourself move away from his ass; it's good, perfect, right. He says your name in all kinds of ways: pleas of want, lust, need, and fear. He's over-whelmed, and you want that. You want to own him this way.

Cole's balls are tight, and his breath is coming in hitching, halting gasps. You think he might come from this, and you need more. You need to push inside him, to claim the space that's yours. You pull away, and he keens, wanting you back. You smirk, jerk him back to the edge of the bed so that it will be easier, and plunge two spit-slick fingers into his ass, watching as he gasps and stares at you wild-eyed and desperate. As you fuck your fingers into him, you manage to open the bottle of lube with your other hand and douse your cock with it.

"I can't wait," you say.

And you can't. You're not sure you can possibly stop now. All of the months of fighting, of pain, of terror— all of the clawing and grasping, and wanting so desperately, it all comes down to now, and you have to go on, move forward, complete this; the fierce need that brought you here rips through you, and you *will not wait.*

Cole's eyes go impossibly wider, but he doesn't move, keening for you, wanting you so much. You pull your fingers out, push his knees up, and aim. He's shaking so hard that your cock jitters over his asshole a few times, but you finally get it right, and you look at his face as you push. His mouth opens and he makes a noise of pain, but his cock jerks and pre-come drips onto his stomach. You press again, and he sucks in air, tensing.

"Shh," you say, rubbing a hand down the back of his thigh. "Let me fuck you." You have to…you need this so much.

"Damon," he says softly, and he exhales long and slow.

You push again, and Cole's almost unbearably tight. Your cock aches, and then Cole just *lets go*, and you slide into him in a long, slow, ecstatic stroke. It's unbelievable the relief that rushes over you, the thrill, the *victory*. It's coming home after a long war, scarred, but euphoric and fierce. Triumphant.

Cole's face is wide-open and vulnerable as you try not to slam into him. It's too good. You hold back from fucking him with the brutal need that's driving you, and you kiss him, breathing in his moans and soft noises, as you slide in slowly. His ass grips your cock, holding you and pulling you in as you push. Cole grasps your back, drawing you down against him, whining in your ear and then gasping in pleasure, arching up to meet you, saying, "Damon, Damon, Damon," like he's never going to stop.

You've never had a loving home. This is what home is. It's pure and it's hot, and it's Cole looking at you like he's come undone. It's collapsing on top of Cole, thrusting into his tight body, feeling him move beneath you. It's Cole's arms around you as you fuck, as you move together, and his breath in your ear whispering your name over and over on half-sobs of joy.

It's over too fast. You can't stop the orgasm that hits you like a car wreck, tearing you apart in ways that are unbearably good. Your mouth is against his, and his heart is pounding so hard that you feel it against your own chest, as you shudder and twitch. You can't keep your eyes open it's so powerful. He claws down your back, and you feel him reach a hand between you, tug on his own cock, and then he's coming, too. His ass clenches your still jerking cock, and he cries out, wrapping his legs around your torso trying to pull you deeper inside.

It's everything. It's *everything*, and you're finally free, finally right where you were always supposed to be.

You're a tangle of limbs and heavy breathing, and Cole's little whimpers as your cock starts to soften. You need to pull out of him now. You kiss his neck and force his legs from around you. You hold the condom in place as you pull out, and Cole makes a sound so sad that you have to kiss him again. The condom slips off in your hand, and as you kiss him, you empty the contents onto Cole's stomach, mixing your come with Cole's own.

"Damon," Cole says, holding you close and tight. There's so much in your name. You kiss his cheek, his mouth, and his hair. There are no words for that. You know. Just your names.

"Cole," you say, and he kisses you until neither of you can breathe.

CHAPTER 7

H ALF AN HOUR later, Cole's trembling and still covered in the mix of their come, but it's not enough. He needs more. He's hard again, and Damon's fingers are fucking into his ass, keeping him open, rubbing over his prostate until Cole feels like he's going mad.

"On your knees," Damon says, shoving at him, and Cole rolls up onto them, obedient and eager. Damon pushes him down until he's got his elbows pressed into the mattress, and his ass in the air. Damon pushes his fingers in again, and Cole bows his head, humping his hips desperately, riding Damon's hand.

"Jesus," Damon says, awe in his voice.

Cole has never felt anything like this. Whatever he'd imagined sex to be, he'd been wrong. This is…something else. This, this is *sex*. This is primal and hard, and he needs it more than he needs air to breathe. He needs it more than he ever needed alcohol. He has to have Damon again, needs him *so much* it consumes him. He can't believe he almost never had this at all.

He whimpers when Damon pulls his fingers out, tempted to turn around, grab Damon's hand, and shove them back in again, but he bites his lip and waits with a pounding heart, thrilled when he hears the rip of another condom wrapper. He throws his head back on a wail as Damon shoves into him hard. Cole's already twisting his hips back to get more, and it's so good, so perfect and beautiful. He's certain, absolutely sure, that he will never give Damon up, no matter the price, no matter the horror that it's cost so far.

Damon clings to his back, riding him so fast and hard that Cole feels like he's being flipped inside out. He's nothing but nerve-endings, good, so good, making him shake and quake, and his cock jerks strings of pre-come onto the sheets. He's always been a romantic, always thought of making love as something sweet, and gentle, but now he knows that making love can be like this—so intense and desperate that he doesn't know where it begins or ends, and he only wants it to never stop. It can be Damon's teeth in his neck, or his own nails digging into the bed; it can be loud and really hot, hard, and scary. It's gorgeous and beautiful. It's everything he wants in life, and it can only be like this with Damon. He only wants this with Damon. And he doesn't care what or who is sacrificed.

Damon is heavy on his back, and Cole's holding them both up as they grind and rut together, until he can't hold them anymore. They fall to the mattress. Cole spreads his legs wider, so that Damon is in him as deep as possible, feeling it in his eyeballs, his teeth, his thundering heart. Cole never knew he's capable of the noises he's making. Every stroke in he feels like he's on the verge of coming, and every stroke out leaves him shivering and wanting.

He begs. He begs like he hasn't since Damon died and he pleaded for it to not be true. But now he's begging for yes, more, please, and Damon, because he's there and it's perfect. He's probably crying, too, but he doesn't know because all he knows is that this is so good, so right, and so intense that it is hard for him to endure, and at the same time everything he has ever wanted.

Damon uses his thighs to spread Cole's legs further apart, getting in even deeper. Cole claws at the bed, digging into the sheets with his nails and his toes, crawling away from how good it is, but Damon jerks him back, and he's shocked, completely shocked, when Damon plows into him again, and Cole seizes up—can't move or shift, frozen on Damon's thrust—and then Cole comes so hard that he can't see or breathe. He hears himself yell, and he's scared for a moment because he's never felt anything so damn good, but then he's shaking and quivering under Damon's still thrusting body, melting into the bed as Damon moves on him. He moans softly, tenderly, thrusting his cock into the mess of his come on the sheets, and then Damon digs his nails in, bites Cole's shoulder, and comes, too, with a sound that makes Cole's toes curl and his cock jerk.

Cole holds Damon's hand as he collapses, panting in Cole's ear. "What the hell have you done to me?" Damon asks.

Brought you back to life, Cole thinks. *Brought us both back to life.*

LEAVING DAMON THE next day is almost as hard as it was the day before, but Cole's sore ass serves as a vivid reminder not only that this is real but also of exactly what he has to lose.

The road to the prison in Bledsoe County is mainly fields and farmland. No one wants to live near a maximum-security facility. Cole remembers when they built the place, there were all kinds of protests from the local farmers, complaining that not only did they feel less safe but their property values had plummeted. It's about two hours from Maryville, and he feels like each mile is too far.

The night before, after they'd finally managed to stop fucking, they'd driven into town, and Cole had watched with a pounding heart as Damon got into the brown Honda and pulled out into traffic. He didn't know how he felt about letting Damon have the car. Some irrational part of him wanted to strip him of it, refuse to let him go anywhere alone. What if Damon were pulled over? What if someone saw him and followed him home? What if he was startled by a buck as he crossed a bridge and…?

"I'm not your prisoner," Damon says when they got back to the cabin, glaring at Cole. "Take off your clothes."

"Come on, Damon! It's dangerous." Cole starts at the button on his pants, toeing off his shoes.

"I am not a child," Damon says, pulling at his own shirt, tugging it over his head and throwing it on the floor. In addition to the glaring red scar down his chest, Damon is now covered in scratches, bruises, and bites. Cole hadn't known he could be so fierce in bed, never imagined it possible.

"I'm just saying it's a risk we don't need to take. Someone could see you! You could get hurt!" Cole kicks his pants off.

"It's called an escape vehicle, Cole," Damon says, coming forward to push Cole's shirt from his shoulders. His face changes as his eyes move over Cole's body. "Jesus," he says, reaching out to touch Cole's chest.

Glancing down, Cole sees that he's as bruised and scratched as Damon is, if not more so.

Damon lets out a soft breath. "I turn into something inhuman when I'm in you. I want you so much."

Cole pushes Damon toward the couch, shoving him down and climbing on top of him, rubbing his bare ass over Damon's jeans before reaching down to unbutton and unzip. "You don't need the car," Cole says.

Damon reaches for a strip of condoms that they left on the couch earlier, rolls one on his cock, and groans as Cole slides down on him. "I'm keeping the car," he says, and Cole gives up, too overwhelmed with watching Damon's face as they fuck to argue anymore.

Now, though, Cole is feeling antsy about it. What if Damon leaves the cabin? He said they needed more condoms. He said they needed more food. Cole countered that he'd bring them with him when he came back, but Damon is stubborn, and Cole knows it. It's part of what Cole's always loved about him. Cole fingers his cell phone and curses that Damon doesn't have a phone of any kind in the cabin.

"I couldn't risk trying to buy a cell phone without identification. And with what money? Besides, what am I going to do with it?" Damon asks when Cole confronts him about the lack of ability to communicate when they're apart. "Order pizza?"

"You like pizza," Cole says.

"I like no one knowing I'm here more. I'm dead, remember?"

Cole sees the signs for the prison and slows down. He's not only nervous about Damon, but he's pretty torn up about seeing Grandpa. It's been a long time, and he swore back then that they were done, that he'd never see Grandpa again. It's felt good all of these years to stick to that promise. But he knows what he has to do, and his grandfather's history cannot be allowed to take the center stage here. Cole must retain control of the situation. Everything depends on it.

The prison is intimidating—concrete and grim. The

barbed wire and armed guards on watch towers leave him with a sour taste in his mouth. So he clenches his ass muscles to feel how sore he still is, a reminder of why he's here, and he pushes his hand into his coat pocket to feel the stone.

"Come on, Cole. Stay focused," Cole says to himself. "Go in. Don't give him an inch. Get what you want. Get out. You can do this."

His phone rings as he pulls into the visitor's parking space close to the entrance. It's Rosanna. Cole can't take the call. Not now. He pushes the 'ignore call' option and drops the phone into his pocket next to the rock.

The check-in process is frustrating. Now that he's here, he wants to do this and get it over with, but first Cole's asked to put all of his personal belongings in a small bowl and to walk through the metal detector. Putting the stone heart into the bowl feels really wrong. He keeps it close at all times for a reason, and Cole keeps his eye on it as he walks through the metal detector.

"Is there something special about this rock, Mr. Hart?" Cole has brought his birth certificate and driver's license, which shows his full name, as proof of his identity.

"Yes," Cole says. "I'd rather you didn't touch it."

He knows as soon as the words leave his mouth that they are just the excuse the guards need to pick up the rock and examine it more closely. A rage burns in his gut as he watches them hand it back and forth to each other.

"Assholes," he whispers under his breath.

The guard's eyes narrow, and his hand goes to his gun. Cole's heart thump-thumps in his chest, and he's washed over with a cold fear.

"Never mind, Peters," a voice calls.

Cole turns to see a man in a white button-down shirt, sleeves rolled up to his elbow, and a stern expression walking toward them. "Mr. Hart has an explanation, I'm certain."

Cole says, "It's a rock. Nothing else. It's important to me. That's all."

He stands tall, ignoring the rush of adrenaline in his veins, trying to play it cool, because he almost blew it. And over what? A rock? Damon is what matters. The rock is dispensable now.

Cole swallows. "Just a rock. It was a gift from someone I love. Someone who died."

"We all have things like that, right, Peters?" the man says. "Warden Madison," he says to Cole, sticking out his hand. "Now, I believe we have some business to take care of?"

Cole nods and takes the rock back from the guard. It feels different. Not the same. And when he puts it back in his coat pocket, he knows he doesn't need it anymore. If he has to, he can let it go. He has Damon's heart to care for instead.

The room the warden has chosen is close to the main office, and Warden Madison says that he'll bring

Grandpa in shortly. Cole supposes the room might be bugged and there are any number of other dangerous possibilities. But the warden seems to have a healthy respect for the money Cole has plied him with, making it clear in a scraping way that he has always endeavors to make Grandpa's life here as easy as possible. He says it as though Cole is going to mete out some payback or declare a vendetta if he hasn't seen to that. Cole lets Warden Madison believe he has that kind of power. Besides, after today, he will.

The room is small. There are no windows and there's only one door. The table in front of him is gray metal, and the chair is incredibly uncomfortable, but Cole relishes the pain in his ass, closing his eyes to think of Damon's face when he comes, of the heat in his eyes, and the low, slithering hotness of his voice.

Cole doesn't have to wait long. He opens his eyes as the door slides and Grandpa is led in.

"Cole," Grandpa greets him with a wide smile and very short hair. As they unlock his cuffs, and he rubs his wrists, Grandpa reaches out to him, saying, "I can't tell ya how often I prayed that this day would come. I'm so glad to see your face, boy."

Cole glances toward the warden, who nods his head and leaves, closing the door behind him.

When Grandpa moves toward Cole with his arms still out, Cole shakes his head in warning, and motions toward the chair across the table. "Have a seat, Grandpa.

This isn't a social call."

"I didn't think it was," Grandpa said. "Everything about this is strange, ain't it?" Grandpa asks, sitting down opposite Cole, an expression of pride on his face. "How'd you get in to see me so fast? Maybe a bribe, Cole?"

Cole doesn't answer, waiting for a moment to get his bearings. His grandfather is exactly the same, if a little thinner, and Cole remembers in a flash all of the things Grandpa has done over the years to the people Cole loves—to his mom, to his dad, to Rosanna, to himself.

Grandpa leans forward with an intense, earnest expression. "Don't waste our time together. Tell me how I can help you, boy. What have you gotten yourself into?"

"You'll never believe it if I told you, so let's just stick with what I need you to do for me, and what I'll do for you in exchange," Cole says.

He's not weak. He can do this. He knows that his grandfather will agree to do everything that Cole asks of him.

COLE STOPS BY Hop 50's after going to the drugstore to get more condoms and lube. They haven't used the entire package from before, but it's a pain to have to stop whatever it is they're doing to find one. If they have enough, they can keep some everywhere. Not that they'll be in the cabin for much longer.

While he's waiting for the chili and hamburgers to be packaged, Cole calls his mother, makes some inane, cheerful small talk, and tells her not to worry about the guy he's seeing.

"It's not serious, Mom," Cole says. If that's not the biggest lie he's ever told, it's definitely one of them. He's glad to have the conversation by phone so that she won't see his face. "I don't know why Rosanna is in such a fuss about it. He's just a nice distraction before I move. And no, I haven't decided just yet where I'll be moving to, but once I do, I'm not going to wait. I'll be out of here."

Cole accepts the packaged food and tosses some bills on the counter. It's too much, but he doesn't have time to deal with change, not when his mother is in the middle of a patented egged-on-by-Rosanna freak-out.

He sighs. "I know—I know that you want me to think this over, but Mom, I've done nothing but think for two years. I need to act. This is for the best. I promise."

He walks toward Southern Grace Coffee. The instant stuff in the cabin is making both he and Damon jittery, and he's determined to return with two steaming hot coffees for both of them, and some real ground coffee to make for tomorrow.

"Rosanna's so dramatic. It's not like I'll never be back," he says. "Every important event, I'll be here."

He doesn't know if that's true. He's not entirely sure

if he can risk it. It seems to cut both ways. If he doesn't make appearances in Maryville, then his sister might get worried and come looking for him, or worse, send his mom to find him.

If he does, then he'll be away from Damon, and right now he can barely handle ten hours of that, so he's not sure he can possibly learn to stand longer. In some ways, walking away from all connections seems more dangerous than if he keeps the ties, but maybe he can learn to stretch them to a point that the risk is minimized, if not negligible.

His mom's telling him now all about how she and his dad just want him to be happy, so he takes the opportunity to say, "Mom, this will make me happy. I know it. Rosanna has to let me grow up. When you moved away, she started treating me like her own child, but I'm not. I'm a grown man, Mom. I know you, at least, trust me."

He feels a little guilty saying the words. He *needs* her to trust him, because otherwise, he'll have to go with Plan B, and that includes losing everything.

He hangs up on her just as it's his turn to place his order at Southern Grace Coffee. He's getting anxious now, fretful. Damon has been waiting for him for *hours*. He needs to get back, feel Damon's skin, hear his voice, and put his head on Damon's chest to listen to that amazing, strong heart.

The door to Southern Grace Coffee opens, and Cole's heart drops.

"Cole!" Emily calls out.

Cole wants to kick something. He doesn't have time for this. He has to get back to Damon.

"Emily!" he answers, putting on false cheer and hugging her tight. She smells like candy-scented perfume and the cold winter air.

"Cole, I am so proud of you," Emily says, pulling back to hold onto Cole's arms and smile up at him.

"Wow, thanks. Glad to hear it. But…why?"

She bats at his arm. "Why? You know why! I'm so happy for you, Cole! This is what Damon would have wanted for you!"

Cole blinks at her and feels his stomach sink. "Michael," he says.

"What?"

"Michael told you." He feels sick. He'd hoped he could trust Michael. It's going to be a risky part of the plan but an essential one all the same. He supposes that it's better to know now before he's revealed too much.

"*What?*" Emily slaps his arm again. "No! Of course not! It was Rosanna. And then I ran into your dad at the Kroger and he confirmed it. Oh, Cole. I'm so glad. Just so happy for you. Come on, sit down here and tell me everything."

Cole's palms are sweaty now. He can't believe this. It's like a joke, a bad dream. He glances toward the door, wishing for an escape. "Emily, I can't. I mean, I have to go. I'm…meeting him."

Emily's eyes light up. "Right now? Oh, Cole."

She's like sugar and spice and everything nice right now, and Cole feels a creeping horror climbing up the back of his neck. She has no idea. She can never have any idea. He's in love with her boyfriend's killer. He allows Alex's killer to fuck him, and love him, and he's willing to do anything to keep him safe. She would never understand it if she knew. She would be terrified. Horrified. Sickened. Cole shivers with the weight of his knowledge.

Emily says, "At least tell me who it is? Rosanna and your dad said you're being all secretive." She grins up at him, and it's so cute that Cole wants to respond in kind. "But we're best pals, right? So, come on. Out with it. I won't tell anyone if you don't want me to."

It's Damon, Cole thinks. *It's the best thing that's ever happened. It's a miracle. And he killed your very own Alex, Emily. It wasn't on purpose, though. He didn't mean to. He didn't even know. Crazy thing, huh?* Oh, God. He can't say that. He can't say anything. This is exactly why they have to leave, and the sooner the better.

"I…uh, it's just a guy I knew in college?" Cole winces that he sounds so unsure. "I don't know where we stand right now. You know how it is. I just want to keep it to myself."

Emily looks a little hurt, and Cole wishes again that he were a better liar.

"Well, okay then," Emily says. "Good luck.

And…you're doing the right thing."

Cole swallows, and his chest feels tight. Doing the right thing. The right thing. Emily has no idea, and for that matter, neither does he. How is this possibly the right thing? And yet it is. He feels it in his bones, in his body. He feels it when he comes, and when he wakes up to Damon's sleeping face. He feels it when he touches Damon and smells Damon's skin.

"Thanks," he says. "Hey…listen, um, I just want you to know…I love you. And, uh, Damon? He really loved you, too. And Alex. He'd never want to hurt either of you."

"I know all of that," Emily says, frowning. "The feeling was mutual. But listen, don't think about Damon. He'd be so happy you're moving on."

Cole hugs her again, a lump in his throat. He kisses her cheek.

"What's that for?" she asks, laughing.

"For Damon," Cole says. "He'd want to if he could."

Emily's face falters again, her joy for him flashing to worry; Cole knows that she's realized now that he hasn't moved on any more than when she last saw him after all. "Cole?"

"Just feeling sentimental," Cole says. "Don't worry about me."

She smiles, but it's not as sparkling, and she waves him off. "Okay, then. You go on. Meet up with your hot new paramour. I can wait for details."

Cole waves and has to resist looking back. The thing is, if what Grandpa has set up comes through, Cole probably won't be seeing her again. He won't have time.

✕

"SO, YOU THINK you can trust the man who used you as a drug mule," Damon says, gobbling down the dinner Cole brought like he hadn't had food in days. "I don't think I can."

"Didn't your mother ever tell you it's rude to talk with your mouth full?" Cole asks.

"No. She was too busy trying to figure out how to de-gay-ify me to pay much attention to my chewing habits."

"Oh," Cole says, and it feels like a heavy thud. He knows about Damon's rough childhood. They'd bonded over it originally: his trauma at the hands of his grandfather, Damon's at the hands of his religious mom. "I met her. Your mother. After your death. At the funeral."

Damon shrugs. "Does it matter now?"

"Oh my God, Damon," Cole says, and he wants to crawl over and get into Damon's skin, to love him hard in every way, so that Damon will know that he always deserved more love than his parents gave him. He deserves it even now after all that's happened to Alex. "Of course it matters."

"Who she was to me, what she did? It was quite

literally another lifetime," Damon says.

"I know—but you were just a kid."

"Lots of crap happens to kids. Neuro-trauma from shaking injuries, brain tumors, divorcing parents…being used by a drug-trafficking grandfather as a mule in a cross-border deal. Life's unpredictable. May as well get used to it when you're young. You did."

"And look how great I turned out," Cole says. "A depressed mess with an undead boyfriend, and, oh, hey, I've just engaged the help of said drug-trafficking grandfather who used me as a mule before getting busted and put in prison. I'm a prize."

"Don't forget that your undead boyfriend is a murderer. I think that adds a certain…je ne sais quoi."

"We really shouldn't think that's funny."

"And yet you do!" Damon says.

Cole takes another bite of chili, letting the spicy heat of it warm his stomach. They'd made love when he got home—fucking Damon calls it. Cole doesn't mind. The way that Damon looks at him, he knows what it means, that it's not just sex, and that it's never been like this for Damon before, either. It's making love.

"Grandpa suggested plastic surgery," Cole says softly. "He says doctors can meet us at the plane so that it can be done as soon as we touch down. He says that it'll make it safer. More secure."

Damon munches at his burger, swallows the coffee that wasn't nearly as piping hot as Cole had hoped once he got back to the cabin and they'd both achieved orgasm. Damon shrugs. "Seems like I fought pretty hard to get this body, and it's pretty inarguably hot. But what the hell? Change me up."

"You wouldn't mind?"

Damon rolls his eyes. "If you'll still want to fuck me, I don't mind."

Cole minds, though.

Cole told Grandpa no. No way in hell. He loves Damon, and if the day comes when they have to take that route, then fine, he'll accept a Damon who has a different nose, a different chin, and brown contacts in his eyes. But until then—no. He wants him just like this, the man that he's wanted to see for so long. He doesn't think he can handle it if Damon's face is taken from him again so soon.

Cole says, "We can do that later, if we need to. Why go the most extreme route to begin with? It might not even be necessary."

"It's surgery, chemo, and radiation, versus surgery alone."

"Not a doctor, remember? Not following."

"It's the conservative plan versus the aggressive plan," Damon says. "You're choosing surgery alone. Cut out the problem areas and hope that we don't have to destroy the good cells along with the bad."

"I just want to see your face when I wake up in the morning. Not some stranger."

Damon looks at him, evaluates his expression, and says, "Sentimentality never does anyone any good."

"It's important to me. Imagine waking up, looking over, and there I am looking like someone else entirely!"

"Is he hot?"

"Damon."

"Fine, I get it," Damon says. "We'll take the conservative choice for now. But I'm not giving you up, do you understand? If it means changing my face and calling myself Ralph, then I'll do it. Nothing will keep me away from you."

Cole's chest is tight, and he gets to his knees, crawls the short space to Damon's lap, and buries his face there, breathing in the scent of Damon's crotch through his jeans. "I think you've already proven that enough for two lifetimes. Let's hope we don't need a third."

CHAPTER 8

COLE HOPES THAT once they're out of Maryville it won't be so difficult to convince his sister that he's okay, so she'll stop harassing him. She's called twice since he's gotten back to the cabin, both times to "check in," and is obviously unhappy when Cole tells her that he's spending the night with his friend again.

"Cole, you've never been secretive about the men in your life," she says.

"Man. There was just one."

"Exactly! That's why it's worrying me. Is there a reason you don't want us to meet this guy? Is he in the closet? Is he *married?*"

Cole replies, "Rosanna, you're letting your imagination run away with you. It's nothing like that."

No, it is *so much* more questionable than that.

"Then why don't you bring him to dinner tomorrow?" she chirps. "I can make sure Dad is there, and invite Emily, she's your best friend these days, right?"

"Rosanna, I already told you. This isn't that kind of relationship."

"What kind of relationship is it, then?"

He groans and says something he never imagined saying to his sister. "A sexual one."

Her disappointed sigh and the lie of what he's said bothers him, but he has to get used to it. From now, everything he says to her will be laced with lies. Rosanna is going to be eternally disappointed in him.

"Cole—"

"Rosanna, I'm a grown man. This is my choice. I'm not risking my life or doing anything wrong." *Well, not exactly.* "You have to let me go."

Hanging up the phone, Cole sees Damon sitting on the couch watching him with great interest as he pops potato chips into his mouth. "Looks like the old bastard was right. Blood *will* tell," Damon says chewing noisily.

Cole narrows his eyes at Damon. "And that means?"

"Clearly your sister gets the dramatic streak from your grandfather. Meanwhile, you got your father's romantic streak."

"Damon, please. She's worried about me."

"So, she doesn't want her sweet little brother getting defiled by some unknown monster." Damon puts the chips aside and starts to unbutton his pants again.

Cole is a little surprised that they even put clothes on after the last time. It seems like they can't keep their hands off each other long enough to make the effort worth it. Cole knows it's wrong, but some part of him can't help but thrill at the lengths Damon has gone to in order to get to him, the monstrosity of it shouldn't be a turn on, and yet…

"I can't say that I blame her," Damon says. "I've done some very dirty things to you, and I intend to do even more."

Cole swallows. "And you *are* kind of a monster."

"A monster who's going to steal her little brother away and never give him back." Damon licks his lips, pushes his jeans down around his thighs, and motions Cole over. "Suck me."

Cole falls to his knees and swallows Damon's cock, sucking and choking on it as Damon tugs on his hair and fucks his face. "Mm," Damon says. "You're so good at this, sweetheart. You're so pretty when you do this for me."

Cole shudders and starts tearing at his own clothes, trying to get them off without taking his mouth from Damon's cock. He opens wide, pressing his tongue along the underside, and rubs his own cock through his jeans at Damon fucks into his throat.

He's just getting frantic for more when Damon jerks his head up and away, pulling him up for a gentle kiss to bring the passion down to a simmering yearning. Cole gets his pants down around his knees and then curls up next to Damon on the couch, kissing and letting the moment drag out. They've been so heated since they found each other again. Now, tasting Damon's mouth, slowing it down, it's the first time that he's not been too frenzied to really explore.

Cole's hand slides along Damon's transplant scar with long, slow strokes, and Damon shudders, asking, "Why do you do that?"

"Guess I'm kinky, 'cause I think it's hot."

Damon kisses Cole's neck, and then slides down to suck Cole's cock into his mouth.

Damon's unbearably good at this. Cole rolls his head back on the sofa and breathes as slowly as possible, trying to make it last, draw it out, because his balls ache from coming so much the last few days. Yet he can't stop wanting more—more of Damon's mouth, his hands, his cock. He wants to touch and fuck and come again. He isn't sure, though, how long they can keep this pace up. It seems impossible, and yet he doesn't think he'll ever tire of it.

Damon pulls off, and Cole grabs his hair and tries to push him back down.

"Shh," Damon says, thrusting Cole's hands away. "Let's do something else this time."

Cole's cock jerks at the thought of something new, something he hasn't done yet with Damon. He doesn't know what it is, and he doesn't care, but he trusts Damon with his body, and he'll give him everything and anything that he wants.

"I want you to fuck me," Damon says.

Cole swallows, and his cheeks flush hot. He looks down, and he can't believe that he's embarrassed, after all that they've gone through, and all that they've done in the last few days.

"What?" Damon says. "You…don't want to top?"

"I don't know," Cole says.

Damon narrows his eyes and lifts Cole's chin for a gentle, reassuring kiss. "It's a good thing I'm back from the dead, then. It's about time you tried it."

"We really have to stop making jokes like that. It's disrespectful."

"Right," Damon says. "Because being respectful will make it not true that my heart swallowed him whole. Never mind. Forget that. Listen, you're going to love topping, and you'll be good at it, too."

"What makes you think that?" Cole says.

"I'll be your teacher, obviously."

"How do you know I'll like it?"

"Hot, tight, slick. On. Your. Dick," Damon says. "Trust me. You'll like it."

OH, COLE THINKS. *Oh, God.* This was something he should have known about. How could he have not known?

Damon's on top of Cole, riding up and down slowly. Damon's right. It's so hot, so tight, so slick, and Cole *should have known*, and he doesn't understand why he can't stop thinking that over and over, like a mantra that keeps him grounded.

Damon's body is gorgeous—and except for the scar on his chest, and the scratches and bruises that Cole has left, he's pale and sculpted. The lines of his shoulders and his taut stomach making Cole want to bite and mark him. He doesn't know if it's because he just got Damon back or if it's something about the two of them together. The way they crash against each other so hard and fast stuns him. But everything about Damon and his body makes Cole hungry, possessive, and he wants to swallow him whole, and mark him all over.

Now, though, Cole's the one who feels swallowed, who feels like he's being tugged into Damon, body and soul, and he's riding that bliss so sweetly, rocking his hips up into Damon's tight, hot body. Holding onto Damon's hips, feeling him squirm down for more of Cole's cock, it's amazing. It's beautiful the way Damon takes him in. Like Cole belongs in his ass more than anywhere else in the world, like it's a given, a force of nature, and no one would should be surprised by it, even though Cole is. Cole is so surprised.

"Good?" Damon asks, and his eyes are focused on Cole's face, soft and intimate. No one else will ever see him this way if Cole has anything to say about it. This is his. Completely his.

Cole nods, his tongue unable to even form a yes, because Damon's sliding down and twisting his hips, and, *oh God*, it is so good.

"Yes," Damon agrees, and he grabs Cole's shoulders as he rides. "Now, flip me over and fuck me."

Cole blinks. Oh—okay. He can do that. He can absolutely do that. He grips Damon's hips and rolls them both on the bed. He's on top now, and Damon's knees are bent up on either side of him. It's different, and it's good, and he can thrust more easily, rolling his hips, shuddering as his cock is squeezed by Damon's tight ass.

"Don't be gentle," Damon says. "Fuck me hard."

Cole lifts up on his hands, gazes down at Damon's body curled up beneath him, glances down to where his cock is half-buried inside, and he rocks in harder, and then he slams in. The friction on his cock shivers out over his body, growing, expanding, until he's got his face buried in Damon's neck, almost sobbing with bliss.

Listening to Damon's deep grunting noises, Cole thrusts hard and fast, gaining speed and momentum, rushing faster than he wants toward orgasm. He tries to back it down, but can't—his body is in control, and he's fucking Damon so hard that his teeth clack together, and Cole's eyes roll up in ecstasy.

Cole is shaking and saying things, he doesn't even know what, but he's making a lot of noise, and Damon hums underneath him, soothing sounds, like he's trying to calm Cole, to help him stay in control, but he's really not able to do that right now. Not with Damon's legs around his waist, and his hot voice in his ear, and his hands caressing Cole's back as he moves in and out of

Damon's ass. He's just not going to last. He *can't* last, and he strains to stop it, but there's no use…

He bites down on Damon's shoulder as he comes, shaking in Damon's arms, groaning against Damon's skin.

"There," Damon says. "There, just exactly that."

Cole pants and shudders still, but he realizes that Damon didn't get off. He's pretty sure that he's supposed to see to that. He reaches between them and tries to grab Damon's dick, hoping that he can be coordinated enough to jerk him off.

Damon pushes his hand away. "I have plans for that."

"Mmmphm?"

"Your mouth, and then your ass. I'm not finished yet. Got it?"

Cole nods against Damon's shoulder, licking at the mark his teeth left there. They have all night. And soon, they'll have years stretching out in front of them. There's no rush.

Cole's still naked and very tired. He's never had his balls tied before, but Damon did it earlier to help make things last, and the resulting orgasm had nearly knocked him unconscious. He's not sure that he'll be able to come again for a week, though he knows that Damon will definitely try.

He traces the line of the heart transplant scar of Damon's chest again, closes his eyes and lets himself think of Alex, to remember the last few times he'd seen him, how afraid Alex had been, how off and strange. And now—now he's been making love to Alex's body, only it isn't Alex's anymore. Damon has carved himself out if it, and Alex is…gone.

Cole knows he should force himself to think of this every day. To honor the loss. To consider the pain and torture that Alex went through. It's terrifying, and yet he can't stop the fact that right now, curled up next to Damon, Cole *simply does not care*. He has Damon. That's worth everything to him. He knows it's wrong, but he can't feel any differently. He has no regrets.

Wow. Is it possible he's finally done with regrets?

Cole traces the scar again and says, "When you died, I spent a lot of time thinking about all the things we never got to do."

"Like fuck," Damon guesses.

"Yeah," Cole says. "That was at the top of the list. But there were other things, too. Like seeing a movie together or taking a vacation somewhere far away."

"Good news, sweetheart," Damon says. "Your dreams can now come true. Next week, we can see any movie you want at whatever theater we can find in whatever place we end up in. And the rest of our lives will be a vacation far away from po'dunk Maryville,

Tennessee."

"Yeah," Cole says again, but he's still sad. "But that's not all. I mean, there are other things too that I always wanted with you. Sexy things like to take you to the Farmer's Market in downtown Knoxville, or to have you at our family Thanksgiving, to see you carve the turkey—"

"Carve the turkey?" Damon repeats slowly. "Is that sexy? It doesn't sound sexy."

Cole laughs and kisses his chest, moves up to press another kiss to his neck. "It's okay that I'll never have those things, though," Cole says.

"Yeah?"

"Because we'll see the sunrise on the ocean together, and we'll fuck our days away for our vacations, and—"

"Fuck? Not make love?" Damon puts his hand on Cole's forehead like he's taking his temperature. "What's happened? Are you okay? Where's the sweet, romantic boy I fell for?"

Cole pinches Damon's side. "Dr. Black, you're obnoxious."

"Come on, it'd be kind of scary if I wasn't."

"True," Cole yawns, and he snuggles in close, tugging the soft sheets around them. "Two more days and we'll be gone."

"Good riddance," Damon says, rubbing his hand up and down Cole's back in a soothing rhythm.

Cole hums sleepily and after very little time, drops into a dream of sunshine and beaches, and a Damon who doesn't fade away when the morning comes.

COLE SHUTS THE door to Michael's office and sits down across from him. Michael looks up from his work and says, "I've been expecting this, boss kid."

Cole nods. "Tomorrow is the day. I haven't told my family yet because I wanted to avoid a big scene. And I haven't told Emily, either." Cole pulls a note from his pocket. "This is my goodbye note to her. Please make sure she gets it after I've left town."

Michael nods slowly fingering the small white envelope, and then sticks it into his pocket. "I will."

"So," Cole says. "I need a favor from you, Michael. It's not comfortable, and it's not pretty. It's something that you'll have to keep to yourself for the rest of your life. You can't tell Emily, or my father, or my sister, or anyone at all. There's a life at stake. My life and everything that's most important to me. If you can't promise this, I understand, but I need you to tell me now."

Michael sighs and runs his hands through his hair. "Boss kid, I don't know what to say. I think the world of you, and I believe in you. But this…keeping secrets…"

"I understand," Cole says, and he's disappointed because this will complicate things, but he can figure something else out. He stands to go, but Michael puts out a hand.

"Wait. Okay, I'm in. Whatever you need."

"Why?" Cole asks. "You don't have to do this. Your job here, taking over for me? That's secure."

"No. That's not why. I've never seen you like this," Michael says. "You're—different. And I don't understand why, but you seem like you know exactly what you're doing, and where you're going with your life now. Even though I have no idea what you're up to, I…I completely believe in you."

Cole smiles and he knows it's a sad smile. It's not his usual faked joy, just the truth. "Michael, before you met Emily—what would you have done, what would you have given up for your wife to not be dead?"

Michael's eyes go sharp and worried. "Cole—"

"I'm not crazy, I promise. The thing is I feel like I've got a second chance, you see. Michael, I've fallen love."

Michael's face changes to bewilderment. "In love? So fast?"

"Yes. Here's the thing—we have to leave the country. Tomorrow. I can promise you this: this man, the one I'm in love with, he's not dangerous, and he's not wanted. But we can't stay here. And no one can ever know that I left with him. As far as Emily goes, as far as my family goes, I am alone."

Michael stares at him.

"It's a matter of life and death, Michael."

"Say I agree to this. Why do you need me to know the truth?"

"As my man on this side, the one who protects me and mine, who lets me know what's happening in Maryville, and keeps me abreast of potential surprises in my life—either visits from family, or gossip, or worried friends like Emily. I need you to be my mouthpiece here, the one who keeps it all as legitimate as possible. Can you do that?"

"Yes," Michael says, and he sounds absolutely certain, which surprises Cole a little.

"You're sure?"

"For you, I'm sure."

"Thank you. Here's what I'm risking by trusting you," Cole says. "My life, his life, and any connection I might have with my family or my past. I don't want to lose everything, Michael. Call me greedy. I guess I am. I want to have him, and I want to have my family, and without someone like you to watch my back, the chances of that are nil."

"You've had enough grief in your life," Michael says. "You deserve to have it all."

Cole smiles, fond and tired, and shakes his head. "I won't have it all. I will have everything that matters, though."

Michael nods and stands up to shake his hand. "You have my word. I'll protect you no matter what."

"Thank you," Cole says, and he pulls Michael into a hug. "You're a good man. I told Emily, too, you know."

Walking to the parking lot, Cole's amazed at how

quickly things have changed. He hopes he's chosen the right person to trust. If not, then the aggressive option might not be avoidable after all, and Cole is so tired of being the one to lose.

YOU TOUCH THE brown paper envelope that Cole brought back. Inside there's new name for you, along with a passport and a birth certificate to verify it. There's a new set of educational credentials that make you grind your teeth and snarl about inferior institutions, and a long line of rewritten history that will allow you to do something with your life other than screw Cole silly, so long as no one checks too closely.

"Which they won't," Cole says.

And since people are usually idiots, you agree.

"Tomorrow," Cole murmurs with a tone of awe in his voice.

"Yep," you say, reading over the information again, committing it to memory. "Dr. Red Alistair and Cole Hart. Did you have to reference my ginger childhood?"

"I didn't choose the name, Damon," Cole says. He's distracted. You can see that he's not happy, not as eager to press into this unknown future as he was this morning curled in your arms. He's got the stone you left for him in his hand, and he's flipping it over and over, back and forth, studying it intensely.

He says, "Do you ever think that maybe none of this is real?"

"About every ten seconds," you say. "Why?"

"I don't know," Cole says, and he puts the rock down on the table. "I just wonder if it will ever start to feel real."

"When you're at work and someone's made a multi-million dollar mess of something, and I call to say that you need to come home to give me a blow job before my next lecture at whatever community college I'm teaching at, it'll seem real enough."

"And if it doesn't?"

"We'll be unreal together?" you ask, aiming for romantic. It's a stretch, but Cole makes you want to try.

Cole grins, so it's worth it, and he says, "Sounds like a plan."

He's adorable, and that makes you want to do dirty things to him. You want to teach him how to be even more depraved with you.

"You know what you haven't done yet?" you say, walking toward him with slow, predatory intent.

"Um, no?" Cole says and he kind of squeaks the words, so you know he's already half-hard for you.

"Dr. Red Alistair," Damon says.

"Oh, right."

"And he's never done Cole Hart. What will Red think of him? Hmm?"

Cole's mouth twists into a smirk, and he says, "He's

kinda pushy."

"Yeah? Show me," you say.

Cole shoves you back until your legs hit the sofa.

"He's kind of a jerk," Cole says. "Uses criminals and their drug money to get his own way."

"I like it," you whisper.

"Suck me," Cole says, grabbing your hair and pulling you toward his crotch.

You grin and open his pants fast, taking his cock out and jerking it slowly. "Like this?" you ask, giving him a hot look.

"No," he says, and grips your jaw, forcing your mouth open enough to press his dick inside. "Like *this*."

You chuckle and suck him in, and, okay, you think Dr. Red Alistair can love Cole Hart. Though when Cole comes, his dark brown eyes staring down at you with love and devotion, you're still Damon Black all the way through.

APPALACHIAN RAINBOWS AND Hardiest Hearts are the easy parts. Cole's been grooming Michael for a while for the work, and he's ready, willing, and completely competent. After signing a few legal documents that his lawyers drafted, Cole hands the reins over effective immediately.

The family is the hard part. Rosanna is the hardest.

She stares him down with eyes like darts and she tells him, "Don't think I believe you. Something's not right."

"Maybe once I've sent you some presents the fish in Denmark won't be so foul?" Cole asks.

Rosanna shakes her head and then hugs him. "Just be happy, okay? If you're happy, then that's all that matters."

"I will be. I promise. Plus there's the internet, and email, and I really will come visit." If he can make himself leave Damon. Though, admittedly, that's a very big if.

The goodbye with his sister is emotional, but somehow it isn't as difficult as saying goodbye to his father; maybe it's because Cole sees Rosanna as the biggest threats to his happiness. If she tries to investigate, or check in, then operation conservative plan must become operation aggressive plan, and losing Damon's face could be just the beginning. Because there is *nothing* Cole won't sacrifice to protect Damon now that he has him again.

Speaking of, there's one other phone call to make before he can consider himself free. He waits until he's alone by the waterfall, ostensibly saying goodbye to Damon, to call his mother.

The conversation is short and sweet. When he's done, Cole hangs up the phone and then pitches it into the lake. He has a new number that he'll give to his family when he gets to where he's going.

He takes the stone from his pocket, and he kneels down by the place where he'd buried Damon's ashes once upon a time.

"Damon," he says to the waterfall, like he's done for the last two years. "It's time to say goodbye. I have a new life to begin. I love you."

He places the heart-shaped rock on the dirt where he sometimes leaves flowers. Then he gathers himself and turns back up the trail.

It's time.

When Cole reaches the Knoxville airport, with most of his family in tow, he gives them all one last hug and climbs aboard a private jet funded with money from the trucking business. John, the pilot, will take them as far as Atlanta, where they'll exchange John for a pilot Grandpa has arranged.

Sitting next to John in the cockpit, watching Maryville fade away below him, Cole feels unexpectedly free. He thought he'd feel loss, sadness, or fear, but he doesn't. All he feels is sky—an open, limitless horizon.

Cole feels like a man. He's found a reason to change his world, and he licks his lips, wanting to see Damon, to take courage in him the way that he always can now.

Once they reach cruising altitude, Cole excuses himself to the sleeping quarters. He closes the door behind him and locks it. He rakes his eyes over Damon resting recumbent on the bed, taking in every bit of him. Damon stares back, silent and calm.

"Hungry?" Cole whispers.

Damon pats his stomach and points at the duffle of snacks Cole had stowed along with Damon himself the night before. It's odd for Damon to be so silent, but they don't want to draw any attention or suspicion onto themselves.

Cole crawls on top of Damon's body, kisses his mouth, and shares an intimate smile, needing to feel him close. As the plane mounts higher to rise above a cloud bank, Damon threads his fingers into Cole's hair, and holds Cole's head against his chest. And Cole closes his eyes, falling asleep listening to the powerful drum of Damon's heart.

EPILOGUE

OLD SAN JUAN is sunshine and wind, fort ruins and historical buildings. At first, it's a rush of freedom. The home that Grandpa's former drug-running contacts helped arrange for them is spacious, freestanding, and private with a view of the sea. They make love for days, in every position, and every way imaginable. It takes a while, but it gradually dawns on them that this life isn't going to disappear. They're both here for good. With that understanding, they cut the sex back to two, sometimes three times a day, and actually leave their new home to explore the markets and restaurants.

Despite his complaints about the sun, and the tendency for his skin to burn, Damon clearly has a thing for the water. Cole's never imagined that Damon could be as peaceful as he is when he's standing on the balcony in the morning, looking at the sunrise on the ocean, sipping coffee, and saying nothing at all. After an even longer while, their life is rich and busy, full of each other and their work, and these moments in the morning are often the most peaceful of the day.

Sometimes, Damon grumbles about the loss of his career as a doctor, but in the end he accepts the role that Grandpa and Cole have arranged for him: he takes a teaching position at the Universidad de Puerto Rico, Recinto de Ciencias Médicas. He uses it as an endless source of stories to fuel his life. Cole loves it. He can listen to Damon recount the horrors of dealing with students for the rest of his days and be happy. Because it's Damon, and he's not dead, so it's pure bliss.

Cole focuses on building a new leg of Hart Trucking operating from moving cargo of Arecibo Harbor. Still, he keeps his profile low, preferring to let his newly hired CEO do most of the public work so that he can stay out of the press.

Old San Juan has a different pace of life than either of them have experienced before. Truth be told, they never quite fit in here. Not Cole with his small-town Appalachian ways, and not Damon with his too-fair skin sheltered under hats that Cole forces on him to prevent the burns he's prone to under the hot sun. It's clear that they're considered outsiders by the locals who get to know them at all. Cole has often heard neighbors wonder at Cole's odd habit of calling Dr. Alistair by the moniker "Dr. Black," and he laughs, saying it's an inside joke when anyone dares to ask about it.

There are the occasional scares. His mother threatens to visit but accepts Cole's suggestion that they meet up for a weekend in Miami instead. Damon isn't allowed to come, obviously, but they text every few hours, and Cole feels that Damon's safe to alone for such a short time—so long as he doesn't mortally offend anyone—and probably even if he does.

Fending off Rosanna isn't as easy, and there is an awkward week when Damon stays in a hotel near the university and Cole hosts his parents in their home. Damon bitches about it as he unpacks his stuff from the boxes they'd hidden in the garage during his father and Rosanna's stay, saying, "Next time, *they* can get a hotel, and *you* can go stay with them."

Cole doesn't think there will be a next time. They seemed satisfied by what they saw, and neither his sister or his father like the beach or tropical heat. So long as he's doing well, and seems happy, he suspects they'll forget all about worrying over him in time.

It takes a few years, but Cole does find the strength to leave Damon to return all the way to Maryville for Emily and Michael's wedding. It seems strange, unfathomable, even, as he drives into the town that it was his home for most of his life. He'd imagined that his heart strings would be tugged, and he might find it hard to leave again. Instead, he has no desire to stay. His heart is elsewhere, and he grits his teeth and grins, acting as though it is a huge joy to be home, enduring the moments until he can get back to Damon and the life they've built together.

The day before the wedding, Cole meets up with

Emily in Southern Grace Coffee. She's happy, and it causes Cole only a moment of guilt when he thinks that she seems happier with Michael than she ever did with Alex. Their meeting is short. It's hard to talk to people when his life is so full of things he has to hide. Still, it's good to know that she's doing so well, and he looks forward to telling Damon about it.

Appalachian Rainbows and Hardiest Hearts are now Michael's babies, and Cole doesn't bother to even stop in the offices. He'll see Michael at the wedding, and they'll talk about work, and give each other knowing looks about the rest of his life. Looks that will probably lead to fodder for gossip. Folks will probably talk about Cole's unrequited crush on Michael. He knows from Emily that the rumor is that's why he left town. He couldn't care less.

On a whim, Cole drives up to the cabin in the woods where Damon had stayed and finds it in disrepair. Everything is as they left it: condom wrappers on the floor by the bed, the ashes of Alex's journals in the sink, and a film of dust over everything. It seems unreal. Impossible. Untrue. It doesn't fit in with the life he leads every day in San Juan.

When he leaves, Cole closes that chapter in his mind. He doesn't think he needs to honor it anymore. It doesn't do anyone any good or change anything at all to remember.

Cole survives the wedding, and with all the focus on

Emily, no one seems to notice just how hard he's faking it. He catches the garter, and everyone teases him about when he'll find someone. He shrugs and says, "I'm happy. That's all that matters right now."

The flight back to San Juan is too long, and when he finally gets to their home, he finds Damon on the balcony staring at the sea. He's drinking bourbon, which means he's had a rough day. Cole prepares to be bombarded by a million tales of stupid students, but instead Damon keeps his back turned and stays quiet.

"Damon?"

Cole understands when Damon asks, "Did you want to stay?"

"No," Cole says. "I want to be right here with you." He wraps his arms around Damon from behind, hooks his chin over Damon's shoulder, and feels Damon's heartbeat against the palm of his hand. "Always."

Damon rests back against Cole's chest as they watch the waves together. "Good."

A HEART IS a dangerous thing. You know this better than anyone. Hearts will not be complicit, or quiet. It's a terrible risk to trust a heart.

You've read a lot of Poe since you first woke in a stolen body, alone in a cabin on the outskirts of Maryville, Tennessee, with the shadows of the mountains looming all around. Poe, Shelley, King. You've read the stories that tell the truth of you in more detail than you ever will.

Besides, who would believe you? Is there a man or woman alive who would listen to your tale and not deem you insane? Who would you want to tell? No one. There is only one man who matters. One man who knows the truth.

The truth is hearts are vicious, desperate, and cruel. They want and they yearn, and they'll take what they shouldn't have. You suppose there should be some grief for that, some shame for what is lost in the battle, or some respect for the man whose life you stole.

And yet you have none. Not even a drop. Because you have Cole, and that is all that matters.

Another truth be told, you don't want this for him, this life away from all that made him Cole to begin with. But when he's curled up under you, quivering and desperate, when you're panting together in a sweaty pile of convulsing, trembling limbs, when your heart is pounding in your chest with love and want for him, and he's smiling into your feverish kisses, you can't say that you're sorry, and you can't say that you'd give it back.

Your heart is strong.

You will never give it back.

THE END

Letter from Leta

Dear Reader,

Thank you so much for reading *Raise Up, Heart*! It is one of my favorite stories I've ever written and I hope it felt special to you, too.

Be sure to follow me on BookBub or Goodreads to be notified of new releases. And look for me on Facebook for snippets of the day-to-day writing life, or join my Facebook Group for announcements and special giveaways. To see some sources of my inspiration, you can follow my Pinterest boards or Instagram.

If you enjoyed the book, please take a moment to leave a review! Reviews not only help readers determine if a book is for them, but also help a book show up in site searches.

Also, for the audiobook connoisseurs out there, many of my other books are available in audio. I hope to eventually add my entire backlist, including *Raise Up, Heart*, to my audiobook roster over the next few years.

Thank you for being a reader!
Leta

Book 1 in the Home for the Holidays series

MR. FROSTY PANTS
by Leta Blake

Frosty former friends get a steamy second chance in this Christmas gay romance!

Can true love warm his frozen heart?

When Casey Stevens went away to college four years ago, he ghosted on his straight best friend, Joel Vreeland. He hoped time and distance would lessen the unrequited affection he felt, but all it did was make him miss Joel more.

Home for the holidays, Casey hopes they might find a way to be friends again. But Joel's frosty reception reminds Casey of just how hard he had to fight to be Joel's friend in the first place. It's going to take a Christmas miracle to get past that cool façade again.

Joel isn't as straight as Casey believes, and his years of pining for Casey have left him hurting and alone, caring for his abusive father and struggling to get by. Unable to trust anyone except his rescue dog—and with no reason to believe Casey is interested in him for more than a holiday fling—Joel's icy heart might shatter before it can thaw.

Can Casey and Joel's love overcome mistrust, parental rejection, class differences, and four long years apart? *Mr. Frosty Pants* is a stand-alone, Christmas gay romance by Leta Blake featuring a virgin hero, childhood friends-to-lovers, second chance romance, and steamy mm first times.

tion and true love. This story includes some angst, some steam, an age gap, and, of course, a happy ending.

THE RIVER LEITH

by Leta Blake

Amnesia stole his memories, but it can't erase their love.

Leith is terrified after waking up in a hospital bed to find his most recent memories are three years out of date.

Worse, he can't even remember how he met the beautiful man who visits him most days. Everyone claims Zach is his best friend, but Leith's feelings for Zach aren't friendly.

They're so much more than that.

Zach fills Leith with longing. Attraction. Affection. **Lust**. And those feelings are even scarier than losing his memory, because Leith's always been straight. Hasn't he?

For Zach, being forgotten by his lover is excruciating. Leith's amnesia has stolen everything: their relationship, their happiness, and the man he loves. Suddenly single and alone, Zach knows nothing will ever be okay again.

Desperate to feel better, Zach confesses his grief to the faceless Internet. But his honesty might come back to haunt them both.

The River Leith is a standalone MM romance with amnesia trope, hurt/comfort, bisexual discovery, "first time" gay scenes, a second chance at first love, and a satisfying happy ending.

shifter omegaverse, with alphas, betas, omegas, male pregnancy, heat, and **knotting**. Content warning for pregnancy loss and aftermath.

Gay Romance Newsletter

Leta's newsletter will keep you up to date on her latest releases and news from the world of M/M romance. Join the mailing list today and you're automatically entered into future giveaways.

letablake.com

Leta Blake on Patreon

Become part of Leta Blake's Patreon community in order to access exclusive content, deleted scenes, extras, bonus stories, rewards, prizes, interviews, and more.

www.patreon.com/letablake

Other Books by Leta Blake

Any Given Lifetime
The River Leith
Smoky Mountain Dreams
The Difference Between
Heat for Sale
Stay Lucky
Stay Sexy
Omega Mine: Search for a Soulmate
Bring on Forever
Angel Undone

The Home for the Holidays Series
Mr. Frosty Pants
Mr. Naughty List

The Training Season Series
Training Season
Training Complex

Heat of Love Series
Slow Heat
Alpha Heat
Slow Birth
Bitter Heat

'90s Coming of Age Series
Pictures of You
You Are Not Me

Co-Authored with Indra Vaughn
Vespertine
Cowboy Seeks Husband

Co-Authored with Alice Griffiths
The Wake Up Married serial
Will & Patrick's Endless Honeymoon

Gay Fairy Tales
Co-Authored with Keira Andrews
Flight
Levity
Rise

Audiobooks
Leta Blake at Audible

Free Read
Stalking Dreams

Discover more about the author online:
Leta Blake
letablake.com

About the Author

Author of the bestselling book Smoky Mountain Dreams and the fan favorite Training Season, Leta Blake's educational and professional background is in psychology and finance, respectively. However, her passion has always been for writing. She enjoys crafting romance stories and exploring the psyches of made up people. At home in the Southern U.S., Leta works hard at achieving balance between her day job, her writing, and her family.

9 7 9 8 8 8 8 4 1 0 6 7 7